WHY SHE WEPT

DICK SNYDER

authorHOUSE

AuthorHouse™
1663 Liberty Drive
Bloomington, IN 47403
www.authorhouse.com
Phone: 833-262-8899

Published by AuthorHouse 11/30/2021

ISBN: 978-1-6655-4508-2 (sc)
ISBN: 978-1-6655-4506-8 (hc)
ISBN: 978-1-6655-4507-5 (e)

Library of Congress Control Number: 2021923675

ABOUT THE AUTHOR

Dick Snyder grew up in a small town, Taft, California, and earned his PhD in history at the University of Colorado. He taught at the University of Wisconsin-La Crosse for 35 years, serving as Professor of History, Director of Extended Education, Chair of the Department and member, Faculty Senate. He retired in 2001 as Professor Emeritus. He may not have seen it all, but he has heard it all: curriculum arrays, individual ambitions, affirmative action hires, departmental survival, faculty fights, and private lives unwound in public.

Writing has always been a part of his life and now his interests have fallen on detective fiction, murder mysteries and the eccentricities of characters who parade through Woodland Park. In his most recent effort, he refocuses his narrative to describe the trials and manipulations of faculty and Dean Sallie Drake, as they struggle with timeless university issues, and murder.

Previously, he published 15 short stories, gathered later into Jonas Kirk Mysteries: The Collection. Three novellas followed: Bingo; Pumpkin Fest; The Marquee Murders. He resides happily in Bakersfield with wife, Linda, and waits patiently for NETFLIX to call.

COVER DESIGN: JIMMY GIBBS

CONTENTS

INTRODUCTION

I have long doubted the appeal of academic life to general readers. It's privileges, writings and foibles too often convey tiresome tones of sacrosanct ideation, immunity to community values and thoughtful superiority. But from time to time, there is a quickening, perhaps a reckoning of real life, and the recent success of *The Chair* suggests an audience.

Imagine a working group of 100 tenured faculty flanked by 200 academic staff and 150 support personnel with Civil Service protection. No one gets fired. Most of them see the same faces and hear of various social, sexual and political misbehaviors for all of their employment lives. Memories last decades. Envies flourish. Resentments run deep and are satisfied with viscous gossip, sometimes violence. Sex gets illicit and common, often with students. Marriages dissolve and re-form. People die. Discovery illuminates. Life gets messy. Faces graduate. Careers are checked. Perhaps it's time for another version of an old story.

While I can draw upon my general life experience in the academy, I want to assure readers that none of the characters described in this piece of fiction have any real-life images. This story is about how things might have been…could have gone…seemed to be.

I want to thank a number of persons whose reactions to all or parts of this story have helped me complete it. Correspondence with Doyce Burke, Maurine Ratekin, Marlene Overton, Amber Jade-Rain, Jerry Mariner and James Parker gave me responses to questions or guided me to sources that proved to be very helpful.

STRICTLY PERSONAL

Sallie Drake reached out, found Suzanna's cheek, still warm, and let her own fingers linger as her mind regained sensibility, detecting the scent of sex and Camellias floating above Suzanna's skin. She touched the back of her neck, slowly tracing her spine down to the rise of her flesh. Repeated as though strumming a guitar. Reached around and rested her hand on that flat belly, her fingers dragging a bit, but still, she managed to trace the petals of a Camellia's tight little overlapping arcs. Felt the tremor. Wandered across her breasts, resting briefly. Sighed. Felt along her ribs, again dragging her own two numb fingers, but noting the exquisite balance between flesh and bone...flexible and strong. How long now, she wondered, has Suzanna been one book end to her life? More to the point, how much longer?

"Classes today?", she asked.

"Jsss...dr...in trnoon."

"Eh? Whisper in my good ear."

"Just live drawing this afternoon."

"Well, I gotta' meet with all of you this morning, then segue over to a Dean's Council in the afternoon."

"Yeah, oh yeah...well, you're a new Dean."

Suzanna stretched, creating another angle of her body, that line from under her arm to the point of her hips. Sallie fixed her gaze on it...became distracted...again. She reached her other hand to loop around Suzanna's shoulders, drew her closer, kissed her eyelids, her lips...took a breath and felt the heat building in her once again.

Suzanna interrupted, "I know you gotta be at all the meetings, schedules, budget planning... but don't forget 'bout me."

"You know what they say, 'Memories make a habit'."

"I'm just a habit?"

"More an addiction."

Suzanna loved hearing that, smiled, reached around to Sallie's face, caressed it, slipped a hand through the medium cut, salted brown, coarse hair on her head, and brought her closer for a kiss... last one of the morning, she thought. In truth, they both needed to be somewhere in about an hour. Touched lips, let her hand roam about one last time, and slid out of bed.

"I'll shower. You relax. I'll see you soon?"

"Yes you will, darlin'."

Sallie relaxed back into the sheets, felt them swish around her with a touch as light and assured as the one she had recently used to caress Suzanna. Keep the feeling, she said to herself. In an hour or so she would walk into an office carrying the weight of her title, Dean, College of Arts, Letters and Sciences, and have to deal with uneven faculty temperaments and unseen interruptions. By five o'clock, she would be less than she was now, much as a tree felt diminished by the constant chipping of a woodpecker family. But evening beckoned, a time of renewal. Woodpeckers. Hmm. She had options...her guy, her woman...whatever suited her taste. She could peck at them for fun. She smiled. Tat-a-tat-tat. Nice rhythm.

Suzanna walked through the bedroom, tossing an air kiss, "Shower's free, see you later!"

Sallie heard the door close, gently, let her mind wander...

So here I go again...new job but old habits. Is there something weird about me? Everyone has personal relationships. Humans connect, sometimes without sex, but more often than known, with lots of meaningless sex. What is it anyway, just a way of satisfying impulses…managing feelings, taking multiple dips into the river. Who does that hurt? Keeping professional life out of private life…that's what freedom is really all about. And who wants to live without freedom. Suzanna's a delight but there had to be more. And now with her bad ear, artificial eye, crippled hand and gimpy knee she was gonna enjoy every intimate moment she could find. But if lovers conflicted with her professional life, her decisions as a new Dean, what then? Problem? She hoped not. Did she need to choose? Maybe later.

But how much later? Dean's had to act; make decisions; forge new ways of doing things. If they didn't, there was no next step. So, is that me? Was "later" about to arrive. She carried new status now, more responsibility, less free time, more tough decisions…and they would affect every face she saw…every department, every faculty, and most of all, herself. What would she do with her lovers? Let them slip away? Lay down new rules? To what purpose? Was she vulnerable? In the end, each was just another face, soft or roughed with beard, a body sleek and round or one angled and thick, a mind to meld or one to dismiss. That seemed to be the sum of it. Love…a nice word but it didn't carry beyond a first tryst and never healed a separation. Now, Dean of a college, she would have to construct a new grid. Her lovers would simply have to understand.

Life was never this tough at North Plains State. Doubt anyone there would recognize her now. She wrote a little, lectured, and hid in her office, but now, two states away, she became reborn…a different creature…confident, assertive and ambitious. She engaged faculty and students in conversations, gently exploring personal dilemmas, often offering advice or directing a way to heal their pain.

She loved reciting the Air Force maxim, "Never worry about the air above you, the runway behind you or the gas back at the field". Good advice to anyone, eh? Problems...just deal with them.

She touched her nose, ran her fingers through thick hair edging her face, felt the roughened leathery skin along her cheeks...paused, grimaced. Not the best, but she had other features too, better ones. She kept her breasts molded high, took pride in her hips, a little thick but inviting, and for years cast an aroma created through a variety of Chinese scents she stole from a lovely red-haired lover back in the day. Now, she favored Suzanna's Camellia.

And what did Middleton College faculty see of her. She walked hallways with purpose, body solid as though carved from stone, smoothed by soap and weighted with ambition. Her presence startled strangers, comforted friends, its edges parting space as needed. She surveyed the campus with a plop-plop-plop conveying her purpose as well as her...well, her tension. Life transitions were one thing. Living the new life was another. She was a certain age now. She felt it, and hormonal changes battled daily with her need to release loaded energies without revealing her secrets. Who could she let into her life? Could she take anyone beyond her bed and share more than her body? How could she find both release and satisfaction? The quest consumed her private reflections, her most compulsive behaviors. All these interior worries swirled about her behavioral choices, and they all came with her to Middleton...but she managed them.

And then, the accident... daydreaming about her lover, stepping right out in front of a bicycle near Eagle Park, knocked "ass over teakettle" as she liked to think of it. Face on the concrete, compressed air in one ear, ruined it...one eye damaged beyond redemption, knee severely sprained...never quite the same...nerves in the last two fingers on her right hand damaged. It shook her to the core and as she recovered, she began creating a new view of her future...something above the department, a dean of something, somewhere, somehow...

and as it turned out, she had only to move her office across campus from one building to another.

A new role. A new challenge. Politics, she knew, were a part of a Dean's world, and in her own way…she grimaced a bit at her history… in her own way, she carried political knives so long and sharp victims seldom knew they had been touched. She still chuckled about the way she had slipped into an colleagues' open office, a despised enemy back in NP State, took a magnet and cleansed his hard drive. She later heard him mumbling about "damn computer crashes". She smiled. Ahh, getting even…so satisfying. It was a skill to learn and a treasure to keep. Politics and sex. A potent combination.

Well, get on with it.

She slipped her plastic support on to the last two fingers of her right hand, allowing her to grasp things a little more easily, and headed for the shower. She walked carefully…did not want that right knee to buckle without its support in place. Kept her bad eye carefully closed to protect it from shower spray, toweled dry, dressed…mild contortions to fix her bra in place…adjusted her skirt length, took a breath and relaxed. Put her hearing aid in place…shook her head lightly…all secure. Well, out the door. Big day. Big plans.

MORNING LIGHT

Comfortable in her new Audi, Sallie trolled through the lot, allowing her good eye to sift through lines of cars until she found her personal parking space. She paused in front of a group of students moving past, 10-12 of them, and let her mind sort through her meeting schedule. First up, a general gathering of college chairs, followed by a luncheon hosted by the Vice-President of Affirmative Action, Gina DiVentis, the mouth of Black and White.

She knew what DiVentis wanted to talk about...hiring more faculty "of color". Not a problem, Sallie thought. Just needed to find vacancies and indicate to departments that she would hire only non-white candidates. That would solve Gina's issue, and no doubt leave departments wondering why they bothered to do a search. Good question, Sallie thought to herself. Departments...small collections of small-minded people staked to a past-date notice and blind to the future. She wasn't. No, she thought to herself, no she wasn't. She was focused on seeing the future...hers.

Then finally, the Chancellor's review session at 4:00 pm. Loved being in the loop.

Stragglers made their way safely onto the grass, one of them glancing at her with idle curiosity. She smiled, inviting one in return. Nothing there...no matter. Easing the nose of her car forward, she squinted a bit, found her name and title carefully lettered on a small sign marking her reserved space. With a small grunt of satisfaction she parked. Here she was. New day. New name. Dean Sallie Drake, child of Indian missionaries, Air Force vet turned educator, now focused on career management, leadership values, personal loyalties, and private relationships.

She sat there, absorbing the title, the challenge, the possibilities, the scope of change she could bring to the college. Loved her prospects. Exhilarating! Reshaping curriculum and challenging faculty to improve their teaching strategies would prove her reputation as a "can do" administrator. She shivered a bit with excitement. Success at Middleton could lead to a provost's position somewhere, another step up the ladder leading to a presidency. For now, Dean of Arts, Letters and Science sounded just right. She would bend faculty to her priorities… create an immediate reputation…and move on. Could she do it? Yep, of course she could. Her own physical limitations notwithstanding, she felt herself on a glide path to a university presidency…somewhere.

She sighed. Opened the door and brought her brace over from the passenger side, swung both legs out of the car and placed her feet on the pavement. Gently attached the hardware to her right leg, tapped her foot a couple of times to let the framework settle, awkwardly rose from her seat and paused to gather her strength.

Grabbed her briefcase with the plastic claw attached to her right hand, closed the car door and moved toward Main Hall. Brilliant day. Blue and white sky. Crisp temperatures. She walked cautiously, steadily, to the front of the building, waited for students to exit and tried to slip in before the doors closed. Got her good leg out there in time to keep the space she needed to enter, but bumped her head sliding through…dammit…that one eye…no depth perception. Impact loosened her hearing aid. Finally collected herself inside the building and approached the two flights of stairs that led up to her office. More challenges.

Fifteen minutes later, she entered her college offices, greeted everyone with a cheery "hello", nodded a cue for coffee to her Secretary, Dottie Zoster, and walked into her office. Closing the door behind her, she paused to admire her desk, visitor's chairs and chatting table. She hobbled over to the large windows framing the campus park. Floor to ceiling glass, tempered and treated to modulate light, framed her view, just as she had requested. Lovely. Her good eye appreciated the quality of light and her bad eye didn't complain.

She let out a deep sigh. Just the brief walk into the general office, glancing at her staff, gave her pause. Did she have the right personnel in place. Dottie seemed a little dazed sometimes, but then, single, young, and a refugee from Moose Lake, Minnesota, she probably found the posturing and demands of self-assured faculty a little unsettling. Still, she had hired excellent staff, bringing in four new assistants, and she sorted out and assigned workloads efficiently.

Sallie breathed a sigh just digesting how much Dottie's work freed her to pursue curriculum strategies and nurse some of the ailments she carried around with her. Headache was the most common...another one had been lurking about all morning...but her eye, that artificial eye, it needed lubricant so many times a day, and Dottie seemed to find new potions almost monthly. Sallie sniffled. Maybe a cold coming on. She turned her chair toward the window, took in the green spaces that lay before her and sucked a few easy breaths. Sunlight caught her face...she felt a tickling in her nose...she knew what that meant... gonna be a big one...and sneezed...so hard it moved the curtains and ejected her acrylic eye out across the chair and on to the floor. It rolled to the wall, bounced and came almost all the way back to her feet.

Ooommph! That hasn't happened in a long time, she thought. Needed a more slippery lotion to keep the tissue from grasping and ejecting her eye when she sneezed. She reached into her purse, brought out the lube and cleaned the orb again. Put it in place. Better.

A knock on the door, and Dottie quietly walked in with a small tray, a carafe of coffee, small carton of creamer, sweet packets, napkins, spoon and cup.

"Thank you, Dottie. So kind."

"You're welcome, Dean Drake," Dottie murmured as she set the tray carefully on the large desk, centering it so Sallie could easily reach the coffee cup with her left hand.

"I always feel my day doesn't really begin until my caffeine kicks in, eh Dottie?"

"Oh, yes. Can't start my day without it. How's your eye? Need a few drops?"

"I think I do, Dottie; I've got some in my purse."

"No matter. I've noticed how much you've been bothered by that dry eye lately, and I found a new solution, *ClearVision*. Created specifically for artificial eye. Says here, *'Lubricates tissue, reduces inflammation. Use as needed.'* Should help a lot."

"Thanks, Dottie," she set the bottle aside, "I'm expecting the chair of the English department to drop in for a quick hello. I may doze a bit, but just send her in."

"Certainly."

Drake nodded as Dottie left the office, reached for the sweet packets and opened two. Dumped them in the coffee. Turned to the half n' half. Gripped the carton with her right hand and tilted it toward her cup. Her grip remained firm, carefully calibrated, but soon too strong for the container's edges. They began to collapse. She poured quickly, hurriedly placing the carton back onto the tray…just in time. Stirred her potion, caught her breath and began sipping and thinking.

How was she was going to energize her faculty? Shifting resources was unavoidable if she really wanted to get their attention and satisfy DiVentis' preoccupation with hiring new ethnicities. But more than personnel changes, she would have to create new rules. They would hate that, but she just had to be insistent, demand more rigorous teaching reviews, a more diverse array of non-white candidates for new jobs, greater faculty time spent with students. And the support staff was far too interested in easing through the day. It needed a bit of a kick in the pants, so to speak. She smiled. She would ignore the groans and evil glances from old-timers, and in a short time, she could show them how much better they could serve students, and if they didn't...well she had answers for that too. Salary could be finessed up or down with a new bonus plan she had in mind...reward a few, promise the rest.

She hobbled over to the bathroom door. "Sallie, Sallie," she murmured to herself, "Don't fall". Once inside, she needed to get that plastic claw working correctly and remove the exterior cast on her leg. Manageable. Still, she bumped her head when she turned to close the door and lost depth perception...again.

A similar routine when she finally left, happy enough to use plenty of courtesy spray. *Note to self: thank staff for having all her personal needs met.* She hobbled a bit getting to her desk, missed the first time as she tried to turn the back of the chair so she could plant herself. Cursed the bad eye and made another effort. Her claw brushed over the leather but failed to catch the edge. She took a deep breath, found new resolve and tried again. Made it. Exhaled. Sat. Relaxed.

She swiveled around so she could survey the grassy quadrangle, marked with a variety of shrubs, trees and concrete pathways offering efficient paths of travel. Small groups of students sat, visiting, a few reading. She speculated on what they were thinking...about life, perhaps about classes, more likely about their social lives. Wondered how many of them got laid last night as well as she had? Smiled.

She closed her eyelid to rest the dry eye. Thought again of the specialized drops Dottie left, turned around and carefully opened *ClearVision*. Removed and lubricated the acrylic, lifeless orb. Placed it back in that empty flesh, blinked...ah, better. Thank goodness for

Dottie Zoster…she was such a comfort…really took good care of her. Felt herself growing sleepy. Relaxed. Drifted.

She dozed. Slumped a little and fell into a twilight. A sudden sharp sound outside startled her, the good eye widened a bit and the claw of her right hand grabbed the arm of the chair supporting her. But there was no following cries or echoes. She gave a quiet "ummphh" and settled into her chair, facing the windows, still upright but head slumping, resting.

Outside Drake's office, Dottie looked up as the main door opened. She forced her face to remain professional, absorbing the physical chaos surrounding Eleanor Rouse, Chair, English Department. Rouse visited the Dean more often than any other member of the faculty, carrying with her the smallest dilemmas, complaining about the most irrelevant issues and somehow appearing to be both at loose ends and fully in control of every complaint. Maddening, Dottie thought, the way Rouse assessed the Dean's office and judged it untidy, even as she herself moved along in disarray…scent overpowering, powder, and wispy hair swirling about her, suggesting chaos, much as that comic character, Hogpen, did. Dottie checked Rouse again as she entered the office, and the image remained. Her hair…gray, frayed and stringy capped a willowy body covered with a skirt too long, decorated with a coffee stained blouse, and a face streaked with random marks of rouge and a touch of running mascara. Rouse glanced at Dottie and remembered gentle conversation with her at the last Christmas party. Gave her another look, a quiet nod of the head. Rouse looked around, noted magazines scattered on the table in front of the visitor's sofa. So disorderly. Sad.

"Is Sallie in?"

"Oh, sure. She has a little time before she meets with the chairs. Just go on in."

Rouse did, opening the door gently. "Hi Sallie, got a few minutes?"

Drake jerked herself back to daylight, turned in her chair, carefully, focused, and welcomed her into the office.

"Hi Eleanor. Come on in and rest a bit. Good half hour before meeting with everyone, then face the Chancellor this afternoon. Kind of exciting being in that loop," she smiled. "So what's on your mind this morning?"

"It's really a small matter, I suppose, but quite irritating."

"Ah, let me hear it. Department issue? Is that it?"

"Well, yes."

"Go on."

"I have two tenured members who are reluctant to take more than 18 students into their classes...something about diluted interactions, impersonal connections, inability to engage them as individuals. I don't know what the fuss is all about...28 students, 21 students, 18 students...for God's sake...just teach 'em, I say. But they are threatening to bring the issue into a department meeting, and I know what that'll mean...a fight, and I don't want to fight with anyone."

Dean Sallie Drake paused, engaged her mental strategies. "Hmmm, that could become a gnawing little problem, Eleanor, but I think there's a way out."

"Eh? What do you have in mind?"

"Meet with the two members and tell 'em to shut up and teach whoever shows up, or start planning to teach night classes the next three semesters."

"They would care?"

"Of course. They have evening activities they would be loath to surrender...family, student organizations, free time to let their minds wander, perhaps even a creative time frame where they can read... and write. They'll hate having to give it up and they'll shut up about enrollments. God forbid the problem should be a lack of students. Don't give them a choice. Just tell 'em, 'teach or change your sleep cycle'…that will solve your problem. Tell 'em you have the support of the Dean…and you do."

"Fine and dandy! God, feels good to have you here, Sallie. Quite a change I must say. Well, I'll get on out of here and see you in a little bit. All the chairs going to show up?"

"They'd better," Drake replied, then repeated herself with an edge in her voice, "*They'd better.*"

PIRANHA

They drifted into the conference room, two or three at a time, a few laggards looking about for a colleague to sit alongside. Chatter spread as they waited for the Dean. And waited. Ten minutes into the hour, Sallie limped into the room, surveyed the faces, mentally counted, and moved toward the end of the large table. The chair of the Biology Department, David Corrigan, jumped up and slid the chair back to allow her to maneuver herself into it. As she settled, she felt his touch on her shoulder as he asked, "All comfortable, eh?"

"Yep, all set, thanks, David."

She took a moment to gather her thoughts. Drew a breath and in an even, gently paced voice, she reviewed enrollments, classroom availability, university budget, empty teaching slots and finally, the topic they had all been anticipating.

"In the few weeks I've been here," Drake began, "It's become clear that we have exceptional faculty and healthy programs in most areas of the college. I've been impressed with your preparations for this semester, especially the way you all took the effort to get curriculum outlines sent to students while they were in lockdown or quarantine. Covid hit hard and you can sit safely in here because everyone is vaccinated. Students will be also if they are to return to campus."

She smiled. No one laughed. She didn't care. Rubbed her own arm softly, still sore a month after the JJ needle poked her. Resolved to get some heat on it tonight. Passed her eyes over each of the chairs, mentally reviewing her thoughts about each. All in all, she thought, a very good leadership team. The question now will be whether they can implement her policies. Thirteen departments...bad omen? Well, here we go.

She took a small breath, glanced around the room, "So, we know we can manage distance learning, but it'll be great to have everyone back in the classrooms. Things are getting back to normal, eh?" She paused, rubbed her good eye gently with her forefinger, then looked around the entire room...a tactic she had integrated into her speech patterns.

"We have a great college, but we lack curriculum balance, and I want to address that. We should be able to jump-start students in moving ahead with their careers and part of this challenge is freeing up more laboratory space so we can provide staffing upgrades in Chemistry and Physics. Those two departments need to provide greater support for their majors and help them complete their curriculum more efficiently."

She paused to let the words sink in, then continued.

"There are funds within the college which could be rationalized to expand labs and get students in Chem and Physics out of here in just four years."

She paused again, looked around the room, saw faces tightening, breaths being drawn, fingers tapping the tables. She caught Dottie Zoster's eye, and gave a single instruction. "Please be sure that you get good notes on this topic, Dottie. I don't want to be misquoted later."

Zoster nodded her head, checked to be sure the tape recorder was rolling, looked back and gave a small thumbs-up to the Dean.

"We need to take resources from some departments and move them into new growth patterns for some others. Accordingly, I am planning to meet with leadership in Biology and Psychology over the next few weeks and find ways to reduce some positions, perhaps even a tenured appointment or two, and use them to strengthen Chemistry and Physics. The National Review Association suggests we improve access to the two departments, and hard as it sounds, it's doable... with committed leadership...and I am committed. You should regard these coming changes in staffing as permanent."

She looked around the table, counting the glances as one chair after another searched for solace, for protection.

"Questions?"

Silence. A half-dozen minds began calculating hazards. Drake might not stop with Physics and Chemistry. Where else might she refocus resources? What might they gain? More alarming, what might they lose? How could they defend student academic needs? How could they protect their jobs? What were their enrollment trends? Why now? Silence. Resistance.

Murmurs finally began to sweep through the room as the hunger for faculty, budget and status swirled through panicky minds. Trevor Coxswain in Chemistry and Gerald Sackmaster in Physics sat back in their seats, quietly enjoying this new portrait for their department's future, confidently sporting smiles in a room full of calculations.

The Chair of Biology, David Corrigan, felt his gut tighten. He could not believe what he was hearing. Sallie had to be dead wrong about her data. He knew he had no probationary faculty, and he sent her a look of amazement. She wanted to fire tenured professors and fill new positions in Physics and Chemistry? Was that it? Couldn't be. But she turned and focused her good eye on the smiles of Coxswain and Sackmaster. *Christ, he thought. She was serious.*

Out of her sightline, Emma Burton, Chair of Psychology, gathered herself. *This was simple bullshit, she thought,* and she caught Corrigan's facial anguish as his mind began winding through the sacrifices his department might have to make. He returned her glance and instantly knew he had an ally. What was Sallie thinking, Burton asked herself? *Psychology...strip psychology of its talent and resources? This was outrageous, a peremptory, savage ravaging of her department, and she would not let it happen. Not on her life.*

Still, no one wanted to challenge Drake's comments openly. They knew how difficult it was to move positions around. Firing tenured professors? Not gonna happen. Dismissing probationary faculty, culling Academic Staff positions, undermining current curriculum... all doable, but difficult, and it usually took a few years to get it done. They would wait...and see.

Sallie sensed their growing resolve. She looked around the room and repeated her plans. "We're going to do this and we're going to do it so it is effective next academic year. I know you're all thinking about delaying, waiting, postponing action, diluting my plans."

She paused, rubbed her good eye again, and let it sweep the room slowly. Let silence reign. Finally, carefully, precisely, she returned to her message.

"You can forget that. I have the support of the Chancellor, the Affirmative Action committee and Gina DiVentis. If we can expand majors and hire more minority faculty, they'll be happy. And if we have two stronger departments...*she paused to look around the room...*I'll be happy."

"One more thing," Sallie filled the silence. "I want every department to revise its operating rules so that they are uniform. Dottie and the rest of my office staff will be sending out the format I want you to adopt. I expect this to be finished in the next three months. There is such variation in the way you all operate that I have some difficulty imagining ways to make the changes I want. So, your challenge, as Chairs, is to follow the structure I'm going to send you and get it approved by your departments. I know there are votes to be taken there, but I'm sure you can make it clear to your faculty that there is no choice...and there isn't."

Silence.

"No comments? Good. Let's get out of here and get to work. I'll look forward to a progress report at our meeting next month. Enjoy the challenge," she smiled.

Sallie tried to get up from her chair. She could not quite get the leverage she needed, and again, Corrigan reached over to assist her. As she gained a grip with the crimped, stiff fingers on her right hand, she was able to push her body up, and as she did, she heard him whisper into her good ear.

"See you tonight, hon."

He smiled. Her body flushed.

TEA FOR TWO

Corrigan plunged. She lunged. He groaned. She screamed. The walls echoed sounds of heightened intensity, the bed shaking in rhythm to their bodies, and in those last, most powerful moments, they each rolled heads, looked for solace as their pleasure turned to near pain, convulsions taking their bodies into realms no mind lock could match. Then quiet, harsh breathing, little gasps to recover respiratory balance, finally a gentle relaxation of muscles no longer strained, the warmth of shared fluids reminding them both of their love-lock and it's importance to their lives. Somewhere in those just passed moments, the connection that had first brought them together pulsed, re-established itself, reminded them both of what they offered, flesh to flesh, and what they enjoyed, mind to mind, whisper to whisper.

Slowly, rational thought began to filter back into Corrigan's head as he remembered a reality that he could not avoid. Minutes passed as his mind began re-engaging real life issues. What in the hell was Sallie thinking, reducing his department, curtailing lab space, shedding faculty, hiring new colors and ethnicities? We weren't the United Nations. Christ!

She moved under him, and he lost his worries again, but not for long. After all, he comforted himself, he was getting older. A second peak and both gasped for breath. He rolled off of her, remembering to avoid her damaged leg, wishing somehow that she could bend it enough to sit astride. He liked it when she rode the pony, but the bike crash put an end to that. So there they remained, two single faculty members treating the other to the balm needed to ease professional needs and fill personal wants. No reason to ever think of it ending, he thought, until now.

A silence began to build. Continue this playful foray or raise something else...staffing? Hell, might as well start in 'cause he could not finesse it, not one bit.

"Sal, I gotta raise some questions about that meeting this morning...just to get a better sense of what you're seeking to do."

"Fire away, my man...I'm thinking your ammunition is exhausted, but you may surprise me...again." She laughed a little, a reassuring bit of joy which he took as encouraging.

"Your remarks about moving staff, cutting lab access for Biology and shifting resources over to Chemistry and Physics...what is that, just a way to get some attention? You're not really thinking of doing that are you?"

She raised herself to an elbow, focused her good eye on his face...a beautiful face she thought...paused...then gently shared her thoughts.

"David, Biology has had a great ride. Apart from History, the department of last resort...and Psychology, a department making personal relativism the standard of acceptable conduct...apart from them, Biology is the giant of our curriculum. It carries more faculty, more students, more space, more equipment, and more dead frogs for sure, than any other department in the college." she smiled.

"You and I both know that surrendering positions to be divided between Chemistry and Physics will prove enormously helpful to those departments. I know that yours will be tenured members, but no university can guarantee positions fixed for life. Every department needs to be healthy by the time of the next assessment review, and right now, some won't pass muster. So, yes. I meant every word. I'm gonna do it, even if it means firing a couple of tenured people."

"You can't fire tenured faculty, Sal. That's what tenure means."

"Well, I can shift programmatic needs within the college and if student numbers don't support my new emphasis, I can get rid of tenured people to balance student opportunity. Takes some doing, but I'm gonna do it."

He lay silent for a time, measuring the tempo of her response. It was steadily paced, reflecting thought and plenty of determination. If she were that serious, he needed to take some caution. Should he make inquiries as a colleague or a lover? Better the latter. Might help make the former a better place to be in the next few weeks.

"Well, O.K. moxie lady…I suppose you have plenty of experience in dealing with obstinance, spending a few years in the Air Force. But are you sure that you want to take on the faculty right away? Maybe give yourself a little more time to settle in. I know I love to feel you settling into a comfortable posture, front or back," he laughed lightly, sent his hand caressing her butt while he kissed her breast.

"I've thought a lot about the timing, David," letting her crippled fingers guide her right hand to his belly, wandered a bit. "It's a hard shove, *she pushed*, but better to do it and let the faculty settle with it than promise changes for next year and leave them wasting a year trying to sink my plans."

"So, it really has to be this year, eh?"

"Yep. As Dottie Zoster would say to her staff, 'Come on…let's finish the job. Get it done!" she smiled as she grabbed his ass and gave it a whack with her crippled right hand. That folded little finger poked him hard, drew a little blood.

He jumped a bit, felt a ball of tension grow tighter in his gut. She really meant it! Christ, how would he be able to sell that to the department? It was one thing to talk about a gradual bending of the staffing curve and connecting it closely to some more advanced programming within the sciences, almost a collegial approach. But this impulse she was trying to sell wouldn't connect with anyone.

She was talking about cutting his staffing by 20%. That meant full professors would be sending more time with freshman, wasting more energy in labs, shortening their leisure time...their research time...he corrected himself. Whatever one called it, they were going to be pissed off...and worse, this was an election year.

He gave that more consideration. He had served as Chair of the department for 15 years now...sort of had it in mind to serve one more term and melt back into the staffing pool. God knows, he didn't want to go back to the lecture/lab assignments he taught decades ago. Not gonna do it. So, one more election, a couple of years teaching an advanced course or two, and he could plan an early retirement.

Sallie's ideas about department staffing were catastrophic, and there was nothing in their relationship suggesting she wanted to work out a special deal for him. She was younger...wondered from time to time why she sought him out...but she did...and never turned him down. Happy to travel with him on professional occasions...always circumspect in public, but he found her smoldering under that cool exterior. He was pretty sure theirs was an exclusive relationship, though he didn't worry about that one way or the other. Committed lovers were rare in the comings and goings of faculty romances... but now she threatened him in a more dangerous way, professional destruction. It might be just a thought now, but she seemed committed. How far would it go? A change of heart, an arrogance that would overreach her grasp? What was next? Who knew?

"You *are* a bit of a scallion, Sal. Gonna be fun watching faculty squirm and wiggle under the weight of staffing changes. Next thing, they'll think you're gonna start changing basic curriculum...or are you?"

"Not now, but David, nothing has changed around this college for two decades…can't believe there aren't some modifications we could make that would help students prepare for their advanced courses, don't you think?"

He stared at her, barely able to keep his loving gaze. If she kept going like this, his life would become miserable…curriculum meetings, filling out forms, defending the status quo…who needed that?

"By God, woman, you are a pip! Got the balls of a burglar, though I haven't been able to lay my hands on them yet." He laughed long and hard. "Well, keep me in the loop. I'd love sampling another serving of you."

"Bring a big spoon, David." She laughed at her own joke, let it tail off to easy silence. Already her mind was on her date next weekend with Suzanna. God, she loved that woman!

BAG IT

Dr. Derek Jackson took the knife firmly into his hand, paused, offered a silent prayer on behalf of his target and slid the edge of the blade carefully, firmly into the skin, the subcutaneous tissue, then muscle, felt it rest on the rib and took it over to the sternum. A clean line... no blood, no surprise. His hand touched the body firmly enough to mark the spot for the other incision, drew the knife again, then made the midline cut from the sternum to the pubic bone. Paused. Stared. Peeled back the skin and took a good look at the lungs, mulling as he did the preliminary report that this teen-aged boy had died from respiratory failure following a sudden infusion of fever, a bad cough and general weakness. Primary physician suspected Covid. *"Well, let's have a look," he thought.*

He felt the lungs, stiff with fluid, paused, cut into the trachea and opened his eyes, startled as he saw the raw, highly inflamed tissue...the cough had been severe indeed, he thought. Heart issues too. Magnifying glass...blood clots by the hundreds. Went looking for more. Gently moved the liver to have a look, found it under assault and the same with the gall bladder and small intestine. Hmmm. Something got after this boy in a pretty aggressive way, producing multiple organ failure and a severe infection. Yet, it was one that surfaced within a few days and led to his death. Hmmmm. Going to be very interested in the blood work. Covid might well be the answer.

He closed the incisions, made his notes, and moved on to his next customer, removing the single sheet covering him, an obese 40 something male whose gut was going to demand some bridge supports just to keep his organs in place. Whew! Jackson carefully drained the body of fluids, made his incision and slipped his hand through the cavity, swept under the lungs and gently pushed his fingers all the way down to interstitial fat, pressed harder. It had to be there. Physical evidence was just that...solid, something to grasp, and he wasn't finding it. A bullet, small piece of lead sure enough, but he had looked at the x-rays closely. It was there. Now, he just had to touch it.

As he pressed through the back fat, searching for the interior lining of the dermis, his mind wandered a bit to the scene of this homicide. An alley behind a series of bars served as the last refuge for his friend here, his passing. What a euphemism. "Passed", he mused. No one wanted to say "died" anymore. Nice words preferred. They deflected thoughts from the irrevocable. Died. Dead. Gone.

Well, he had supervised this pick-up carefully. Bad setting. A sloppy alley full of debris easily mixed with the fragments of evidence he might pick up. Still, even in small portions, they might point to cause of death, or better yet, lead to the killer.

He mused again about the skill of the Coroner to be unavailable when the call of "murder" went out. Seemed to be out of town or in meetings at every call, and it fell to him, the Medical Examiner, to direct the crew, collect screened evidence, precisely handle the victim. Not enough to be responsible for the autopsy, he muttered to himself. Too often he was the on-site director, doing someone else's job. He should probably run for Coroner at the next election.

Examined the idea. Spat into the drain bowl. Nah. No way he was going to be soaked in that political poison. Nope. Would ruin his life. He looked some more, his hand pressing. There was a bullet there. Just had to find it. Lodged in back fat?

Did another sweep. Was he gonna need another x-ray to locate it? Really? That would look pretty foolish. He had the original set in front of him, and there it was. He searched again, his fingers cramping just a little, pressing down again…a small sweep, flattening his hand, feeling a larger area this time. Still nothing. He took his elbow out of the cavity, stood there, taking small breaths to gather his senses and a bit of energy…and thought. He reviewed the pickup. He had carefully loaded his buddy here into the body bag, zipped him up and sealed the tabs for ride to autopsy. Couldn't have lost anything there. Safe trip to the morgue. He and Mike Sergeant, his lab assistant, carefully moved their rider into the overhead x-ray machine. Unzipped the bag, peeled it back and shot the images. Undressed and placed him on the table. And there he rested. Peaceful visage. Maybe it was an easy death…he avoided saying the word "passage". Well, by whatever name, it was a common human condition…we all found ourselves in the last corral sooner or later.

He sighed.

The end came sooner than his friendly traveler here might have wanted. He clipped the nails, swept the body for debris, sampled liquids, made the Y incision and found three of the four bullets that he would list as cause of death. Just one more in there somewhere, one more .38 caliber piece of lead, he hoped. Cause if it weren't a .38 that might mean they were looking for two suspected murderers. One, two? A distraction, he reprimanded himself. He was focused on one… just one more. A conundrum. Bullet in x-ray. Body placed on table. Searching body cavity. No bullet.

Suddenly, his face warmed. A rookie mistake, and he was no rookie. He turned quietly to his assistant. "Mike," he said quietly. "Would you do me a favor and put the body bag back on the rolling table."

"Sure, doc, sure." He moved brought it over and lay it on the metal surface.

"Mike, did I ever tell you that I practiced magic when I was a teen-ager. Thought it would help me learn to use my hands when I became a surgeon."

"No, doc. Never heard that one before…point being?"

"Point being that it's easy to lose things, like visual contact with a piece of a magic prop. Look hard enough, and it will disappear."

"So what is the magic here…something in the bag?"

"Yep, I think so." Jackson reached in and searched a bit, finally felt the interior corners…and there it was by the feel of it, and he took a quick look to confirm…yep a .38."

"Well, damn, Doc. What the hell…how did it get from his body to the bag?"

"Passed through."

"Eh."

"When he was shot, the lead passed through his body, lodged between his back and his shirt. We took an x-ray of the body, as it presented, fully clothed. There was a bullet in the image. Undress him, the bullet falls into the bag. Disappears as it were."

"Oh, Christ. Someone's in trouble now, Jesus!"

"No, no, Mike. Could happen to anyone. Faulty protocol. Send a memo to staff. *After removal, search the body bag one last time.*"

"Easy enough…you run quite a nice little operation here, doc. Clean, respectful, thoughtful…and thorough. Bet it's rare to let an actual homicide slide through as simple, natural death."

"Well, Mike, that's my goal," Jackson laughed, "Affirm natural death and spotlight murder."

He slipped off his gown, mask and gloves, let his thoughts roam ahead to the rest of his day. Paperwork to file, three charts to review, shipment of four of his new "friends" off to morticians. Three hours later, he headed home for supper.

He slipped through the air-pressured doors and out into the general lobby, nodded to the gift shop owner and took the elevator down to parking. Found his Volvo and admired it a bit as he always did. Saw his reflection in the windshield, distorted but identifiable. There he stood, six feet three inches, slender, full head of hair, graying temples. Flesh well exercised as noted by his posture. Age perhaps 45, but he looked ten years younger, he thought. And why not. He knew his medical chart...nothing chronic, good family genetics, regular exercise, didn't smoke, enjoyed moderate alcohol.

He lived a thoughtfully balanced life and his wife, Andrea, complemented it with her interests in creative art, healthy foods, gardening and cooking...oh, yes, the cooking. She served a diverse menu culled from their years of foreign travel, and he simply trusted her expertise in the kitchen to keep his body healthy and fit for the long run. She took care of him, and he liked it.

He wondered a bit whether she were bored, comforted himself with images of her time in the studio, her occasional exhibits, and the enthusiasm she had for their visits with the children. Two families, one in the oil country of California, the other perched on the North Dakota plains, a child being raised in each household. One boy, one girl. Not easy to visit from their home in Cottage Grove, but Lindbergh International wasn't far. It was more a question of time, finding it, freeing it and using it.

Well, nothing to worry about today. Finished in the morgue, feeling good, he could already taste a full-bodied Cab, and an evening with Andrea, sharing their appreciation for what life could give. It could end suddenly, yeah it could, but he couldn't see into anyone's future. Yep, be good to get home.

He passed by Middleton College, thought a bit about its contributions to his community. Fine faulty, good student enrollments, scandal free administrators, he thought, and no reports of exploited students. Fresh, young faces returning with vaccinations in arms... or they weren't going to class. Good marks all around, he mused, and noted familiar figures waiting for a light to change. He slowed. It turned red to him and he watched them cross. The limp of the one told him immediately it was Sallie Drake, newly appointed Dean, and there alongside her, Suzanna Ludlow, Chair of the Art/Theatre Department. He was well informed on Drake's injuries, her crash being the talk of the town for a few days last year. He knew less about Ludlow. He noted they stood quite close to one another, nearly touching hands, chatting in a preoccupied intensity that left them standing until the light changed. Suzanna finally looked up, casually glanced his way, then the other. They crossed cautiously.

Wondered where they were going. He smiled. Maybe a romance there. Neither married, though that was not a litmus test for relationships...he well knew that. Life flourished in various configurations. Live as one wished, he thought, cause there was just one destination for us all. His work on the autopsy table certainly detailed colorful stories, robust adventures, creditable careers, inherent biological flaws, but it all ended in the same graphic he saw every day...flatline.

Drake moved pretty smoothly along-side her partner. There was joy there, Jackson mused, probably a special relationship. Keep the thought, he reminded himself...and headed home.

MIXING PLEASURES

The phone buzzed...again. Derek let it vibrate until finally, a restful silence. Really not in a mood to be caught up in chit-chat and Andrea usually texted. Kept working on his drawing, a landscape of empty parkland framed by empty horizons and soft foliage...a walking trail that disappeared in the distance. He paused a moment, took a look at the perspective, liked it, and resumed. He was an amateur sketch artist, and Andrea kept encouraging him. Creativity is a way to avoid focusing too much on naked bodies, abused flesh and the frozen finality of death, she said. His business presented itself as the end of a journey, never the celebration of a lively future.

Dying...he let his mind roam a bit, gently touching on that failure of respiration that triggered the final breath. Many little disturbances could bring the body to that critical juncture. Sometimes, they were well concealed puzzles. Other times, they presented with obvious cause, occasionally flawed by various forms of violence. Usually, he sighed, he saw the posture of a lifeless body as part of a procedural effort to certify cause of death. The summing up...demanding in its required examinations, findings, weighed data, and fluid analysis... always led to that terse summary revealing why a biological process had come to an end. Routine. But still, autopsy demanded a precise mental reconnection of a functioning organism he had just separated for diagnostic purpose. The Coroner had it much simpler. He could make an on-site call about a death...natural causes, under doctor's care…no problem. But sometimes the scene did not present the way it should, and he sent a corpse on to him, the Medical Examiner.

"Sort it out," was the unspoken order, and he was happy to do so, especially when there were challenges beyond marking and tracing bullet holes and knife paths. Once in a while, some element of a death challenged him, kept him engaged in evening thought. He liked solving mysteries and occasionally, a silent lump of flesh challenged him, gave him a mind bender. He loved that.

His phone. Again. Irritated, he answered, tried to modulate his tone.

"Hello."

"Hi there, Derek, this is Suzanna Ludlow. Got a minute?"

"Oh, hi Suzanna…sure, what's going on?"

"I thought I saw you at a stoplight while Sallie and I were walking yesterday. That you?"

"Yep…out shopping?"

"A little, mostly just enjoying some air and exercise."

"Great day for it," he commented.

"Bet you're wondering why I called?"

"Caught me."

She laughed, "Well, Derek, you're a candid conversationalist. Same style in autopsy reports too, I suspect."

"Caught me again," his voice smiled.

"O.K. Let me get to it. I'm wondering if you would like to visit my life drawing class sometime in the next week or two."

"What? Life drawing?"

She laughed a bit, "Yep…surprised you, eh Derek?"

"You did. Gee, Suzanna, I'm really not sure what I might have to offer. I do a little landscape painting, but never life form…see enough of it at work."

"Oh, that's the point, Derek. I think it would be provocative for my students to hear you speak from the autopsy table…however you choose to do it. I think that'd give them a better feeling for the posed bodies that they are drawing…give them some imagination in creating a faithful or perhaps a fanciful image of the model."

Jackson remained silent. He knew Suzanna Ludlow by sight and an occasional quiet bit of chit-chat when he visited a college art exhibition. Attractive, tall, maybe 5' 10" and shapely…he wondered from time to time if she had modeled in college…almost had to… lengthy limbs, body smoothly shaped and she moved about with a certain peaceful look on her face. It was a sensuous, sleepy-eyed look, absorbing life, love and longing, yet keeping senses balanced. Seeing her with Sallie Drake, in public, didn't necessarily mean what he thought it meant…but likely it did. Lovers. A complication for their careers at the university? Not in this era, he thought, but one never knew…large egos often pressed the boundaries of tiny minds. Was it an attraction between the Dean's flawed body and the near-perfect balance of her companion? Maybe. Or perhaps personal experiences blended into a comfortable dialogue that found additional refuge in the bedroom? Their business. Their lives.

Well, random thoughts even as he looked for a way to avoid Suzanna's invitation. He almost gave her an outright "no", then paused. Softened. Hell, he wasn't doing it for her; he would be doing it for the students and maybe that was reason enough.

"How soon?" he asked.

"Oh, anytime in the next couple of weeks…they're doing very preliminary sketches now…would that work?"

"Well, sure. Let me sort through my current workload and see if I can find something a couple of days out, understanding it could be interrupted by some sudden need of the Coroner, eh?"

"Works for me, guy. I'll wait to hear from you."

"Excellent," he said and closed his phone.

He stood there, pondering whether Suzanna was pandering... looking for something beyond a guest appearance and comments from someone who knew bodies inside and out. She was single and had been so "forever". He'd be happy to be of real service to the students, but the thought remained...was there more to the bargain? Money? Access? Surely not sex. Surely not. Give a talk to art students? Maybe a nice, gentle thing to do. No stress.

What *was* the stress in his life, he wondered? Happily married for years, he found himself well situated in a career that pleased him, nothing boring, nothing threatening. His, he thought, was the happiest of lives.

Was it the job itself? Sorting through bodies and sifting through liquids on behalf of chemistry that seemed to function so well in a healthy body...was it more stressful than he recognized? He knew how beautifully the human body operated...as an organism. But he rarely saw that in his daily explorations. Death...shorthand for failed chemistry... had a way of converting one's daily expectations for living into frightening projections of limited mortality. Was he stressed about anything? He didn't think so.

He explained it all to Andrea that evening over their quiet meal of smoked chicken, green beans, cornbread and molasses. Another balanced menu fueled his energy, calmed his tensions and healed nerves.

"Suzanna just called, out of the blue, really...wants me to give a little presentation to her life-drawing class. I just don't quite connect her interest in my appearing."

"Oh, really Derek," she smiled.

"What?" he looked at her.

"Sometimes you are so dense. You have a reputation for expertise not often found in a Medical Examiner, and you need to remember that she is chair of the Department of Arts *and* Theatre. You can enliven the art of drawing, and she likes to put on a nice show."

"Well, maybe so, but how is that supposed to be helpful to students learning to draw limbs, postures and expressions. I can manage a landscape, but I'm no expert on drawing life form. I just know parts and pieces."

"I doubt that she is looking for expertise. I'm sure what she wants is for her students to know that she is connected to people with status. That would be you, eh?"

"You think?"

"My sweet, naïve husband. Go on into her studio and just give the students some observations about human form in life and death. That'll shock them a little and give Suzanna all the attention she wants."

"That's it...you think?"

"Believe it, dufus."

He grinned. Poured some more molasses and spooned a soaked cornbread into his mouth. Taste buds...working just fine.

QUICKLY

A week more, then two. Finally, a lazy Friday morning. Reports submitted. Meetings over. Casual dress. Banter everywhere. A workday that promised a bit of fun. Sallie decided to make her morning a special time, to renew a connection she kept deeply private, but celebrated with soaring joy in an obscure place: the auditorium.

Constructed in the late 30s, its brick exterior gave credible meaning to the phrase, "Main Hall" and it still carried that special blend of balcony seating and interior spacing that could hold a peace rally in the 1960s or an intimate performance of "Death of a Salesman". Its one nod to modernity was a remarkable concentration of technological power in the projection booth centered at the rear of the sloping main floor seating. A black space to a casual glance, it sheltered projectors, computers, routers, remote hookups, and a superb audio system through which music and reproductions of both great and terrible speeches could be broadcast throughout the void. Within its walls one found secrets recorded in the sanctuary of anonymity, a dark cloak of intimacy that could heighten senses, allow unbounded passions, even tolerate a small scream or two, whatever a private moment might produce.

Rows of seating echoed silence. Pathway lighting offered safe passage, but threw larger images on walls...scattered, skittering shadows as soft currents of circulating air moved a leafy plant, a tethered flag, perhaps caressed a silently moving body.

Sallie walked casually, dragging her right leg along with minimum lag. Coffee time in the office was over. Cleanup underway. People coming and going, and she felt the urge, knew a rendezvous had to be a part of her morning. Lots of worry that week…department chairs whining, the Chancellor worrying about enrollments, dozens of curriculum requests flooding across her desk…and private meetings for an hour each with Emma Burton in Psych and David Corrigan in Biology, discussing staffing, lab assignments and enrollment burdens. It was easier with David since she had access to him in almost any configuration she wanted to frame. But Emma was different. Calm, direct and never one to back away from a conviction, she pressed the issues to the point of exasperation.

"We'll take it up next week, Emma," she finally concluded and sent her away. Told Dottie she was done meeting with anyone and to re-schedule the rest of her day. "Gonna take a break and go hide away awhile," she grunted. "Gotta get out of here." She turned to leave and bumped her leg, her bad leg, against the corner of Dottie's desk. Threw her off balance, nearly fell, catching herself with her bad right hand against the adjoining table. That damn bad eye, she cursed to herself, and in spite of her resolve, the pain from the leg caused her to sound off. "God-damn it, Dottie! Will you move your desk. I walk this path 20 times a day. Get it out of the way."

"I'm so sorry, Dean Drake. I'll get Big Jim to re-arrange the furnishings in here later today. It'll be a lot more comfortable by Monday…it will."

"Small comfort to my leg, dammit, Dottie…and the numb fingers on my hand throb…I must have bent them trying to push away from the desk. Christ, I'm getting out of here for awhile."

As she closed the door behind her, she took out her cell phone. Paused. Classes ending. Hit that favorite number. Answered. She spoke, "Auditorium…ten minutes." She walked with a greater sense of purpose now. She moved down the corridor to the side door of the unseen space, unlocked it. Stepped inside. A deep, dark pocket of air embraced her, immediately bestowing a sense of irrevocable privacy, a secretive placement in which all things were possible.

She paused, waited until she could hear her breath moving softly, letting her eyes adjust to the darkness, feeling the shadowed air wrap itself around her, caress her, quietly easing all discomfort from her knee or her hands. Sight was another challenge…depth perception always a problem. She waited another minute, finally saw the path she wanted and carefully limped her way to the back of the auditorium and into the control room. Guided only by a soft, "nite-light" she entered it carefully and moved the chairs over to the far end of the workspace.

She looked around, drew a deep breath, and began removing her knee brace, then the plastic cast on her right hand. With greater intensity, she gently, provocatively removed her clothing, making sure that her bra and panties remained within easy reach. She caressed her body, feeling the numb fingers hand drag across her abdomen, letting her left hand linger on her breasts, letting blood flow begin its inevitable re-orientation…and waited. Ten minutes had passed. Students were free of classes by now. Where was she? There was need here, pressing need, and she desperately did not want to lose the momentum building inside her.

Then, the quick flash of light as the side door opened, closed just as quietly. All dark. No silhouette to follow, but she could sense her growing closer, could almost feel the heat building in her core as she stared for a glimpse of hair, sniffed lightly for her scent. She heard a soft breath outside the open control room door, and knew all was well. "Get in here" and she did, entering a little breathless, breathing deeply.

She heard the slide of fine fabric as the body disrobed, paused and whispered, "You ready?"

"Oh, God, yes...get over here!"

As though a screen emerged from her brain, her senses now filtered into the touch, scent and breath of her lover, now standing, now kneeling, now exploring her body even as she returned the attentions. Breathing grew stronger, strengthening in waves, deep, then deeper, finally a series of shallow catches, a longer pause, a gasping of deeper air, repeated in cycles...one, two, three and then the blessed interval of gathering, each to her own sense of momentum, but gathering nonetheless...and in that series of spasms and moans, stifled screams really, the fingers that each knew how to control found their way to a launch, a mutual send off that left only the strain of muscles and deeply controlled breathing to convey their transportation...to where, only each one knew...but to that space and placement where senses merged, shook and contracted...once, again...a series of movements that took a minute to ease, and minutes more to subside, allowing breathing to catch itself, and legs to regain strength. They remained close, still caressing, waiting for the eddies of the storm to subside and pass into another memory.

A whisper. "Oh God, tell me again...it's safe...no one knows. Students? I don't hear anything when I'm walking the halls." Students?"

"My Lord no! It's safe. You're just another face in the crowd... milling with students when classes change, and without you I'm just an empty vessel. You know that. I'm just sitting on a shelf, waiting for another moment we can have. Not a word circulating about you out there."

A sigh. "I take a terrible risk being with you...hiding in public places...I don't know why I do this...my age...it's not my nature, and I worry...do people stare?"

"You're safe with me...always."

"If we're caught, I'd be dismissed from the university...that would be awful...my gosh, what would my mother say?"

"You are safe...don't give it another thought."

Minutes hurried by and finally she gave the cue, reaching for her leg brace, bra and panties. Time to rejoin the lives they had just briefly escaped. They re-layered their clothing, adjusted hair and blotted lips. The visitor left first, departing through an auditorium door opposite the one she entered. Sallie took a deep breath, let herself relax, gathered a renewed focus on time, purpose and tasks to solve. She could reform the college, she thought, but she needed her occasional succulent, well, succulents, she thought...and smiled. Well, that's what secrets were for...she smiled...nurturing hidden truths.

SKIN TIGHT

Derek walked cautiously down the hall, seeking a room number, not sure of either its place or his. He wondered again why he agreed to do this...speak to life-drawing classes about the human body when he knew it best in its deathly state. For him flesh was an end point of disease or human accident, maybe mayhem, but a conclusion all the same. Nothing lively about his work, unless one factored in his interest in solving an occasional mystery. Been quite a while since anything like that had come across his table in the morgue.

But he wasn't here today to talk about the eccentricities of body failure, but rather to speak to the human form, and from that word, "form", he found a topic that he thought might work. We'll see, he thought. He found the studio, knocked and waited for Suzanna to open the door, thought again how he might present his little talk, wondered whether she had motive beyond the subject of life drawing, speculated about her connection to Sallie Drake.

Click! The door opened and Suzanna's angular face greeted him with a smile and a caution. "They're just underway, Derek. Slip on in here and we'll chat a bit before interrupting them."

He stepped forward, caught up immediately in the quiet ambiance of shadows and reflected light, and the image of the nude male model standing motionless on a slowly revolving platform. Well, makes sense, he thought, everyone gets a chance to refer to their original vision a few times a minute. Students sorted into a circle with their easels, drawing paper attached, chalk or carbon pencils working softly with occasional glances at the model. He was no stranger to the human body, but still, Derek thought, it seemed a bit vulnerable to just stand there, posed with an arm just so, a leg bent, a back curved, naked and open to inspection for long periods of time.

He took a good look, again feeling relieved that the model was breathing, face unmoving but body clearly full of life. His eyes unfocused on any particular object, neck tilted, hair in place, muscular structure well defined (must lift weights, he thought) and still, so very still he stood. Great stamina, and he took a look at his groin, the mass of hair and the penis and testicles lying softly in place. Sensible he thought. Much as his own male customers presented. He smiled to himself.

"Well, Suzanna, where would you have me stand and what are they expecting?"

"Oh, just move over here near the lectern and get comfortable. I'll give them a few more minutes and then introduce you. Let's see what happens."

"Oh, sure, easy for you to say," he smiled, "I'm the day's diversion… I'll just try to make it a bit interesting."

A few minutes more, and Suzanna quietly interrupted their work, introduced Dr. Derek Jackson and said simply, "He works with the human body and may have some insight into how you might approach your drawings." She turned and nodded to him, and he walked over to the lectern, paused and smiled, glanced around the room…the model was now seated in his own chair, lightly wrapped in a covering. Everyone seemed to be interested in whether he would be worth a listen.

Hello to all of you." *(Boring, hmmm…need to change the tone right away).*

"Have you ever given thought to how your model might look if we just peeled away his skin and took a look at the musculature beneath, the tendons, the ligaments, bone, internal organs all exposed for sight-seeing. How might that appear to your eye." *(Better...he had some attention).*

"I can imagine that the first thing that would happen is that all the orderly placements of the body would readjust. Without skin to hold them in place, organs begin to fall out of place and deteriorate. Digestive forces would extrude the stomach and intestines; lungs would react badly to dry air; joints would soon become cranky from lymphatic fluids leaking away, and the form that we know as human would slowly but decisively transform itself to a mush of flesh."

"Skin is essential to your task. You cannot draw human form without it. Indeed, the health of your model depends upon keeping his own intact. You know the expression, 'Have any skin in the game?' If you do, you know its meaning. Losing the contest diminishes you, leaves you vulnerable, sends you looking for ways to compensate, to get your skin back."

Derek paused to see if he had the connection he wanted and found the return gaze of his audience satisfactory. He took a breath.

"So apart from containment and the insulation skin gives us from a hostile environment what else does it say to us?"

"It is nearly two square yards of covering, about 15% of the body, using 8-10 percent of our metabolism to maintain itself. It creates a boundary, but not a barrier. It interacts with sunlight, absorbs moisture, sheds fluids, controls temperature. It bends, burns, folds, restores itself until decades distort its tension, erode its collagen and leave body form lax, far from the tensile strength it carried in its youth."

He took a look about. Mild interest.

"And what of color, that distinguishing mark that sometimes means person, sometimes pariah? The skin controls social content, supports or decimates individual opportunity, acceptance, status. It can open careers and just as quickly change them...see affirmative action."

Well that connected. Nice to see that happening. Maybe offer them the closer now.

"The skin may appear to be benign, but it's daily activity is as essential as that of the lungs, and when attacked by disease, it can prove as vulnerable as a besieged colon, and just as fatal. Contrary to that old Trump blather, light does not pass through it. It is essentially a surface organ with complex layers, vulnerable, slightly translucent. Indeed, one of the first things we look at in an autopsy is the skin... scrapings, scars, debris, tension, bruising, attachment. It masks revelation, and as a medical examiner, I must penetrate every barrier to a full understanding of a cause of death. Where do I begin? The skin."

He let that sink in a bit, checked the clock now marking about 15 minutes of air-time...and he knew that he had another five minutes to hold them. After that, their minds would wander back to their drawings. Best wrap it up.

"And what do I do next...I start collecting fluids and then proceed with a Y incision and inspection of internal organs."

A groan of revulsion. Fine, they'll remember that.

"I finish with sawing and removing the cap of the head and lift out the brain...weigh it, inspect it for gross injuries, see if the victim suffered from alcoholism or some plaque disease. Shaky, gray brain matter contains the most complex network of information storage and retrieval we can imagine. Everyone has one. Some just function better than others," he smiled

"It is the capstone event of an autopsy, I guess," he smiled. "So, when your model returns, treat his skin as a barrier to the world around him and a connecting link to all his muscle posture might suggest. Let his face be neutral. Find the message in his skin: color, tension, blemish, moisture, tats, wrinkles, and mounds. They tell a tale."

He bowed a bit, turned to Suzanna and concluded, "Thank you all for your attention. I've truly enjoyed this little session."

He stepped away from the lectern to appreciative applause. Saw the students turn immediately back to their work but felt satisfied. Maybe they benefitted from it all. The model stood again, regained his pose and the pedestal began to turn, slowly.

Suzanna glanced at the class, blinked a couple of times and refocused her look...on Derek. What he must know about the human body, she speculated, "Wonder what he could do with mine?" Always a question she pondered in meeting men, even as she mentally reaffirmed her commitment to Sallie. One person was enough. But then, there was always the other gender...hmmm...something to keep in mind.

"David, that was just wonderful...think I'm going to have to take better care of my skin...avoid sunlight more often I guess."

"It all matters," he smiled, "Sun damage is cumulative, but you work indoors for the most part...you'll live longer for it."

"Now, that is comforting, Derek, (*she couldn't help giving him a bit of a sleepy eyed look*)...I like a diagnosis that promises healthy longevity," she smiled. "Thank you again for coming by. See you at the student exhibitions in a month, eh?"

"You will, Suzanna," he smiled, gave a careful nod back to any students still watching, and quietly left the studio. Andrea would be pleased he spent some time here...and he liked to please her.

DRAWING A LINE

"He gave quite a fine little talk," Suzanna murmured, letting a hand slip from Sallie's breast to her groin, felt that little irregularity that always intrigued her, its warmth, moisture, slipping through her fingers. She wondered what that intimate piece of flesh, a quirk of some kind, she guessed, might look like if she drew it. Well, Sallie was uninhibited in most things, but she drew the line at certain visual inspections. Off limits. Suzanna smiled, thinking of the delicious ways she could approach forbidden spots, then pass them by. Always added a little more tension to be resolved.

She passed her palm up through Sallie's hair, traced a line across her abdomen to her breast; her left one was Suzanna's favorite. Sallie took a bit of a deep breath, tried to focus her one good eye on that provocative hand, missed it and closed her eyelids…let herself relax and just feel. Saturday…a respite from the week's burdens and a celebration with a creative artist, and an imaginative lover.

"Suzanna, you think Derek suspects anything about us?"

"I think he does, but I'm sure if he were to worry about faculty affairs, his mind would spin out of control. I think he merely notes what he sees and moves on."

"I hope so," she commented, then took a moment to remove her acrylic eye and breathe on it, poured some *ClearVision* in her hand and rolled the eye in it so it would set more smoothly in that empty socket.

"Doesn't that bother you, Sallie…having that eye sort of floating in your head, no focus, always fiddling with it…makes you look like a bit of a dead cow."

"Oh, it's just a little something to put up with. Truth is, I get more frustrated with those numb fingers on my right hand…sometimes I can't even pick up a sheet of paper without using my left hand…just something about that paralysis that seeps into my other fingers… nerve transmission or something I guess. Makes it damn tricky to hold toilet paper," she smiled. "I should ask David Corrigan about that… in biology. He should know something about nerves and healing windows…toilet paper too," she laughed.

"Well, maybe that's the wrong department. Looks to me like you need a more carefully fitted support for your hand, maybe something in a light ceramic…something I could create for you, eh? Maybe make it a decorative ring with a flaring cradle on each side to support the fingers…something you could flash around. It would divert attention from your eye."

"Hmmm," Sallie let her mind imagine something more distinctive. "Maybe with a lot of color, perhaps a bright background with eye-catching little figurines, maybe little blobs of puddled color. Eh? Or maybe a series of tones that matched the colors of my dildos. An array of something I could just flash it around as a kind of jewelry, eh? What do you think, Suzanna…could you do that?"

"Oh, sure…a bit of a challenge to get the fitting just so, but," she smiled that lovely warm embrace, "sure, I can do it. Give me a month or so."

Sallie took a breath…a deep one and slowly let air out, relaxing her body as she let her mind begin to wander from the pleasures of Suzanna's body to the discomfort of taking control of the chairs of the various departments and putting things the way she wanted them. Where to start? Unlikely to have real problems with Corrigan in

Biology. He'd whine a bit, but she knew from their years of private pleasures that he would do what she needed.

Now Emma Burton over in Psych, she was a different bottle of beer. She presented sturdy, wholesome features and a calculating mind that could make a knife in the back feel like a comfortable scratch. She had tried to catch Burton's eye privately more than once but to no effect whatsoever. What she saw was much the same stare as that of a snake waiting for a moment to strike. Misread her at peril. Truth be told, she enjoyed Emma's company from time to time, but there was nothing sexual about her friendliness, nor anything gentle in her rejection of policy if it didn't suit her.

So, how would Emma take to this strategy...depriving her department of four probationary faculty in favor of Chemistry? Taking two tenured positions out of Biology and sending them to Physics didn't seem too tortuous on its face. David would whine all the way to her breasts, but Emma? No one was bedding her and making a deal. Needed to have some leverage there that would force the issue in ways that put her in a political crunch.

Make the question simple: take my deal or hear a worse one from the Chancellor. That might work. Trick would be to convince Chancellor Worrell to buy in. But he might. He believed there would be consequences if Chemistry and Physics didn't meet the accrediting standards coming up for review. He wasn't interested in a campus crisis, nor were his Board of Directors. Threats to accreditation meant fund-raising troubles. No. He wouldn't like that.

Well, the question for now was: What would Emma do?

Suzanna stirred, looked at Sallie. "Where in the world is your mind, partner. I tickle your butt, scratch your back...nothing. Do I need to push you out of my bedroom and let you cry for help? S'up?"

"Oommmphhh. Oh, hell, those damn Chairs...hard for me to stay away from thinking 'bout how I'm gonna deal with them...damn,

I'm sorry." She reached over and held her lithesome partner in a full embrace, kissed her cheek, her ear and her lips. Suzanna smiled. Everything Sallie offered her complied with full commitment. Their future might be muddled by time and circumstance, but it wouldn't be sullied by another pair of arms. Not ever.

She arose, reached down and traced an oval on Sallie's left breast, then her right, both remarkably full, taut and formed. She thought again, *Sallie girl, you must work those pecs a lot...should bring you into the drawing class and ask you to model for a session.* She stored that thought and offered another, "Now get on out of here and let me calm down and design a brace for those two fingers. Maybe let them do something useful again...soon," she smiled.

Sallie arose, laughed lightly, took in Suzanna's scent once more, Camellias...so light and yet so memorable...and moved over to slip on her clothing. Gathered herself, turned to kiss Suzanna good-bye, misjudged her step, tripped and nearly went down.

"Can you do anything about turning a one-eyed lover into a fashionable Dean?" she muttered.

"I think you'll be surprised. Be sure to lock the door, eh? And watch out for the back porch stairs."

"I'll focus on that," Sallie laughed and quietly disappeared.

PICNIC

Bright. Bright eyes. Bright smile. A bright shiny creek tossing reflections wrapping themselves across his face, embracing rosy cheeks, twinkling blue eyes, highlighting streaked, blonde hair. A picnic. Voices all around, unfolding with as much fun as he could remember. A day in the park, resting near the rushing water, full of lazy lounging, stuffed with food that tickled with treats: ice cream, bratwurst, burgers, deviled eggs, yellow cake deeply concealed below thick, layered chocolate icing. For him, soda pop. For his parents and Elaine and Jed Simpson, beer and a thermos of martinis, pre-mixed. Old friends. A bright day.

He, Ernie Wilson, age 7, wandered the area, sneaking around dense bushes to try and surprise a rabbit, hiding for a moment from the adults, picking up interesting looking sticks. Tested them to see if they broke easily. Snapped a couple and threw them aside. Kept one to fish insects. He finished poking an ant hole and looked again at the stream. Picked up a stone or two...took time to throw them into the creek, or was it a river, he thought? How did one decide? Was it deep? Cold? How wide, really? Was it a river or a creek? How fast was it moving? Where did it end? Could he walk into it and just enjoy cooling his legs?

He looked at his parents, pouring the first of the martini mix, tending the bar-b-que, laughing with the Simpsons as old friends did, spewing little short hand jokes, drawing on other adventures and the edge of adult humor he seldom understood. Not going to ask permission to dip a toe in the stream. He knew the answer would be "no". Quietly walked over to its edge, bit of a fall off from the bank down to the water, and he thought he could just slide over the edge and dip a toe, maybe a foot in the water…just to see how fast it ran, how cold it felt, how deep it might really be. An adventure.

He sat down on the bank's edge and let his legs extend over the short precipice. Looked over his shoulder at his parents again. They were laughing at another joke, swigging a swallow of beer, sipping a martini. He edged his butt over the earth's edge and felt his weight crumple its edge, freeing him to slide right on down…which he did, but faster than he had calculated and suddenly the water which seemed placid from above, spoke a small roar to him and he wanted nothing to do with it. Placed his feet into its current, tried to stand and lost balance. Tried to return to shore, just a step away and could not, lost balance and crashed with a muffled thud into the water. Not a sound.

Only a couple of minutes, she thought later. Just a brief bit of time when she lost track of Ernie. She looked up. Didn't see him. Scanned the nearby woods, the stream, the picnic grounds. Not in sight. A panic, intense fear, she jumped to her feet, letting her beer spill, called his name, "ERNIE! Hey where are you, little guy? ERNIE!"

No answer. Didn't think. Reacted. Rushed to the stream, more a river she thought. Reached the bank, saw the earth disturbed, the footprints into the water, looked downstream and screamed, "MY BOY! MY SON! HE'S IN THE WATER. DO YOU SEE HIM?"

A small collection of young men and a few women, all in their twenties, heard. They looked up, turned around, took a quick step toward the creek. "There he is," one shouted, "My God, there he is. Get him out!" Two of the men jumped into the water, tried to reach the boy, but he floated by just out of reach. They tried to swim faster than the current, but it left them short of their mark. Ernie continued to move along and away, not stirring, not fighting. Another, larger figure from the group jumped from bank to water 10 yards further downstream from Ernie, got there, but the boy slipped from his hands and continued drifting.

"MY GOD!" Evelyn Wilson screamed, "HE'S DROWNING... FOR GOD'S SAKE, SOMEONE SAVE HIM!"

But Ernie floated downstream, out of reach and now out of breath, out of safety, entering quietly into the cloud of death. Tragedy unfolding before the eyes of the innocent triggered guilt surfacing in the hearts of his parents. "SOMEONE SAVE HIM!" Evelyn Wilson screamed again...and again. But no one did. No one could.

And that was the story they gave Sheriff Alfred Monroe when he finally connected with witnesses and the Wilsons. "They could have saved him, but they let him drown," Evelyn wailed. "They just left him to struggle and float downstream...drifting away...away."

"Maam," Monroe began, "Others reported to me how many of them tried to rescue your son. Great effort but a tragic failure. "He paused to choose his words very carefully. "We know Ernie entered the water himself, and right now, we just have no evidence to charge anyone with a crime."

And in that moment of anguish, Evelyn Wilson's heart went up in flames. No! This would not be an accident where inattention could be lain at her feet. No. This was dereliction of responsibility by young men who could have saved Ernie from drowning. And she would see them in court.

"Sheriff Monroe. I want the District Attorney to look over your reports. My son is dead because these party-drinking young people were too drunk to get to him. They let him drown. My attorney will be filing a lawsuit immediately...as soon as we bury our son. All those teen-agers should be in jail!"

Monroe hesitated, cleared his throat and spoke quietly, "Maam...

Mrs. Wilson. What you're saying amounts to a crime…good Samaritan neglect…and if it is what you allege, we are going to have to have an autopsy. Will need to know for sure what caused Ernie's death. Drowning certainly looks likely, but our Medical Examiner, Dr. Derek Jackson, will have to confirm. That will take a few days."

Evelyn Wilson stared at Monroe. "You people are all the same… looking for excuses to make things easy for criminals…they are murderers you know…is there such a thing as 'homicide by neglect'?"

"I'll leave that to the D.A. to sort through Mrs. Wilson. But for now, Ernie will have to stay with us. You sure you want to go this way?

Evelyn Wilson chocked a bit, shook her head, then spoke as best she could get her words out, "autopsy please," and began to weep.

"I'll be in touch, Maam."

Monroe turned away from her anguish, tried to extinguish the knot in his stomach. Autopsy. No telling what would come of it.

GUILT

Autopsy. Derek didn't get many requests to review cause of death. In medical school, it was part of a pathology student's third-year rotation, and he wished it were required for every specialty. Most medical students wanted nothing to do with viewing the results of their handiwork, and he understood that. But, still, nothing might create a passion for accurate diagnosis and restrained prescriptions as much as a good look at what failure looked like. Not just a number. A person.

And now, here was another...a young boy, someone's son...death in a tragedy. Derek understood the buckets of emotion surfacing...a child...a sudden loss...an explanation...a blame. Gonna' be guilt deposited somewhere...maybe everywhere in some transcendent kind of collective regret. But guilt came in different forms: neglect, causation, inattention. Even fate. For how easy it was to deconstruct "fate" and find causative guilt. It's a mess already, he thought, and he better be sure about his report.

He hung up the phone, turned to Andrea, a sudden sign of weariness touching his eyes. She saw it. Braced for the news.

"I'm gonna have to get over to the lab right away. Young boy found dead in Oyster Creek. Some citizen rescue efforts failed, and parents are demanding to know cause of death."

"Are they looking for explanations...or trouble?"

"Probably both. I'm not gonna like this. Really upsetting to have to examine children lost in accidents…such innocence."

"Let me send you on your way with a couple of protein bars and an orange, hon. You may be standing at that table for quite a while."

He nodded, "Sure…yeah, this might take a while." He reached out in a bit of a distracted motion, took the little bag she quickly put together. Caught himself already letting his mind wander. Brought it back and gave her a hug, quick kiss. Life, he thought. There it was right in front of him. Andrea. Thankful again.

"See you soon enough. Love ya."

He backed his Volvo out of the garage, set it straight on the local road and headed for the lab. His mind wandered as he drove… revisited that first stark, uncompromising look at death that lay on that stainless-steel table in medical school. He purposely had avoided looking at the face, concentrating on the larger scene, hoping to find some clinical distancing. But, there it was. A human, aggressively presented with chest propped up for ease of access, a temporary resting place for a lightly bearded, slightly obese male. His white skin now competed for attention with drains, hoses, scales, dishes, tables, syringes and tools…all seeking illumination from the merciless overhead light that ensured that biological truth would be revealed.

Birth…hope…promise. Those were the words that he liked to associate with the human experience. But this final look, the autopsy, startled him. *A* sterile, lonely journey, he thought, but also a satisfying look at the way bodily systems deteriorated on their journey to death. Draining liquids, scraping injured skin, examining internal organs, searching for damaged tissue, cancers, clogged arteries, perforations… every step perhaps a clue to the wear and tear that took a life.

He remembered his first look at the Y cut, the quirkiness that he felt in his gut…such a lethal slice among the living, but here, he quickly told himself, it was akin to a zipper revealing testimony that could be gathered in no other way. The careful look at liver, stomach, lungs, intestines, all perhaps once healthy, but now multi-shades of inert color, starved of oxygen. Then too, there was the opaque, sinister look at tumors, their insistence on entwining within healthy tissue or intruding on space once occupied by a healthy functioning pancreas, gall bladder, colon, or prostate. Those parts made the rounds in all common talk about possible cancers, but he had first look at what language could not fully describe...damage, distortion, engorgement, filament-wrapped death.

Was that all? No, far from it. Under the microscope there was more. Blood tests screened for disease markers and drug abuse, spoke of the flawed chemistry inherent in the red and white cells, carried liquid clues to poisons. *Blood...always a treasure trove of information.* And so it went, a methodical, sterile, thoughtful examination of what a life lived could tell a medical examiner about how it died.

What of the death certificate? He smiled? Half the time, it erred in describing cause-of-death. Literally half. My God! What strategies applied to patients in the name of treatment were aimed wrongly or administered thoughtlessly? Too many. He remembered his first autopsy. Cause of death on the certificate: heart attack. Autopsy produced a different answer: punctured bowel.

How he came to embrace his look into the secrets a human body kept from prying eyes was a story of its own. Not that he felt like a Peeping Tom, but he just wanted to know what seemed to be forbidden information. In medical school, his teachers hammered home the maxim, "look...and learn", and conventional wisdom demanded a good review of a body in any kind of circumstance. But today, even in the medical profession, curiosity about cause of death had deteriorated to the point that an autopsy rarely occurred unless death might be a matter of criminality.

He could not have disagreed more. Autopsy was a way to satisfy a critical medical query...what truly caused a death?

Hmmm. Why didn't people want to know more? Why didn't the medical profession want to oversee its treatment outcomes more insistently?

For surviving family, he could see the reluctance. *Aunt Jessie's dead...not much to do about that now. We'll bury her, mourn her, and move on.*

But this case is likely the reverse. *They are thinking "our boy's dead and someone is to blame".*

He ran that disturbing statistic through his mind again: *Almost 50% of death certificates cited a cause of death which was in error when reviewed by autopsy.* He held on to that percentage as an act of faith. These parents just wanted to know what caused a tragedy. His boss, Coroner William White, didn't often call for an examination post-mortem, but when he did, Derek remained sensitive to the possibility that he could correct a death certificate, and he remembered a few family disputes finally settled based upon his discovery of a true cause of death. Maybe the same issue here.

Well, here we go.

He gowned his body, gloved his hands, masked himself and began inspecting the boy's skin, looking for bruises, cuts, evidence of any systematic abuse. Some bruising on rear of his skull, he noted, presumably from being tossed about in the stream into which he fell. He drew fluids from bladder, veins, arteries, abdomen, made the Y incision and had a look at the lungs. Inspected both halves. Felt no evidence of water in there, each being pliable, healthy and unpolluted.

So. The death certificate citation on cause of death was wrong. *The boy did not drown.* Derek paused, decided to look at the brain. Somehow, for some reason, the child stopped breathing. He gently removed the skin from the skull, inspected it and found light signs of bruising embedded in its underside. Carefully, he removed the bone cap, then the brain, and gently probed and moved it about, looking for clots or signs of exterior force...finally found it...an embolism well pronounced and defined on the hypothalamus.

He had his answer. The boy fell into the stream, hit his head on a rock, rendering him unconscious and immobilized. Bleeding in the brain affected his autonomic nervous system, ending his breathing. But...he didn't drown.

He completed his notes, sealed the collected vials of fluids, carefully sewed the chest back together, replaced the brain, glued the skull cap, gently layered then sewed its skin covering. Well, he sighed, the family can mourn without worrying about a stranger's guilt. Of their own responsibility, well, they would just have to deal with that. He grimaced.

He checked the lab schedule, saw another autopsy scheduled for the afternoon...an adult male, age 68. Fine. He'll get to it after lunch.

He unwrapped himself from his lab clothing, washed his hands, disinfected his face and back of his neck, called Andrea.

"Derek? Everything all right?"

"Quite so. Thinking of having lunch. You interested?"

"Where?"

"Adagio's."

"You buying?"

"Yep. You leaving the house?"

"Can't get out of here fast enough," she laughed and he echoed it. Marriage. Never better.

Derek arrived first. Ordered a light, white wine for her, a Cab for himself. Andrea entered less than 10 minutes later, smiling, quietly loosening her light wrap and giving him the look that took him anywhere she wanted him to go. She glanced about the room as she sat down. He poured her wine. She sorted through the bread loaves for balanced slices, crispy crust, solid centers, glancing casually about the room, then posed a question for Derek.

"You notice that group of women three tables over, on your left?"

He glanced around and looked them over.

"No. Something special there?"

"Well, at first I thought they were just celebrating a birthday. Lots of laughing, few little private jokes and general focus on the blonde... youngest of the group, I think. Notice how her hands seem to make little circles in the air, open and close, as though she wants to explain something in greater detail...you see that?"

"I do not."

"Look closer. Notice the brunet with the short, fashion cut...the way that she looks at everyone, then waits for them to look back at her...and they don't."

Derek took a series of quiet looks. Tried to see what Andrea described...and failed.

"What you trying to tell me, lady."

"I think this is a wedding shower lunch. The bride-to-be is the brunet, but she is not really the center of attention. The blonde is, and she is making sure that she remains the focus. I'm willing to bet that within the next 15 minutes, the bride-to-be is gonna have a melt-down and lunch will be over. Time me."

Derek was constantly amused at the way that Andrea could do this...read the body language of people and understand it far beyond what might be said aloud. She had escorted him out of more than one tepid reception when she read the room and knew that there was nothing being offered that would benefit his career or satisfy her conversational interests. Didn't take her long either.

"O.K. Three minutes gone by. See any action."

"I can hear a voice beginning to get a little shrill...another is trying to shush her...things are getting tense."

"I'm seeing nothing," Derek said, softly.

"Just wait."

Suddenly, from the table, the brunet, bride-to-be simply stood up and said, "Karen. This is really embarrassing. If you need an audience, go find one somewhere else. I appreciate your efforts to put this together, Dorothy, but it's neither fun nor special. I'm heading home. Rest of you can have a good time singing praises to the Blonde Bitch at the end of the table. Adios."

She walked out, tears now streaming down her face, weeping mixed with anger, rejection lancing her joy. Dorothy trailed after her, whispering comforting words and offering an occasional supportive touch on the shoulder. They passed Derek and Andrea's table, trailing the scent of light perfume and lighter wine. The remainder of the group, four in number, watched them leave, looked at the blonde and settled into the next round of chat and chew. Luncheon was over. Serious gossip now underway.

Derek took it all in. Sent a private glance of appreciation to Andrea. "My God," he thought, "She should teach a class on 'Reading Body Language'." He'd sign up.

He raised his glass to her, air-kissed a compliment and settled in to enjoy yet another hour of life with her. Andrea laughed. No end in sight.

SALLIE DRAKE PAUSES

Sallie walked into the office, limping but energized by the morning challenge. It's been a month now, she thought. Time to pronounce the inescapable plan she had for Psychology and Biology. She paused briefly at Dottie's desk.

"You can bring me my coffee now, Dottie, and when Emma Burton and David Corrigan show up, smile warmly and let them know it will be a few minutes. I'll call when I'm ready."

"Can do. Coffee'll be ready very shortly."

"Would you mix the milk and sugar this time, please?"

"Of course."

Sallie Drake smiled a tight line across her face, adjusted the hearing aid in her right ear, touched and lightly massaged the closed eyelid covering her false eye, noted the slight headache hanging around all morning, dismissed it and moved on toward her sanctuary.

"Thank you, Dottie."

Once in her office, she left the door open enough to hear important office gossip, yet not enough for anyone to just walk in. Seeing it that way, she knew, would irritate both Emma and David. They were there on demand and without leverage.

She smiled, moved carefully toward her desk, sidled around and gently placed herself in her swivel chair. With a sigh, she slowly turned it toward the tinted, floor to ceiling windows, letting her good eye survey the park below, noting the healthy foliage, enjoying the sight of students lounging on green grass, visiting, studying, listening to music...just taking moments of rest between classes. She like seeing that.

Dottie knocked gently, "Coffee's ready, Dean Drake."

She turned around, motioned her forward, indicated she wanted it placed on the center of her desk and dismissed her with a curt nod of her head. She pursed her lips and sampled her cup...carefully. Ahhh, just right. Simple woman, Dottie was, and she always knew how to mix a simple pleasure. She turned again to enjoy the view.

As she slowly sipped, she began to think about Emma and David. They weren't going to be happy with her, so she might as well move directly toward the sacrifice she planned. Then, send them on their way to sort through it until they realized they had no way out. They were going to lose positions in their departments, and that was that.

She knew how to finesse a controversy, but in this case, she had leverage. No need for subtlety. She held the power. She could order obedience, once again reminding herself that change was the currency one used to gain advancement. She didn't want to look too far ahead, but just two or three years of leadership here, and she could start applying for a provost's position somewhere else. Let the losers settle into a new culture. Let the next administrative era deal with them. She would be gone...maybe off to New England, or out there in Colorado, perhaps a small private college in the Pacific Northwest, someplace with real stature. She shuddered a little anticipating her future. It would feel so good.

But first, Burton and Corrigan. Out in the receptionist area they sat, chatting, waiting for the call, knowing that they were being kept in place through calculation rather than necessity. Games.

Corrigan murmured an aside to Emma, "Sallie's going to play serious hardball. You ready?"

"Damn right. She's so infuriating, so certain, so pompous. She needs a good pricking, and I have my pointer," she pointed to her data filled document. "Unless she wants to eat her young, she's gonna have to back off...*the bitch,*" she whispered.

Corrigan smiled to himself. Well, he had something that could prick her too. She was gonna be disappointed in his response.

"What you carryin', Emma?"

"Data?"

"Star Trek?" He smiled.

"No. Hard data. Student data. Instructional data."

"Think that'll be enough?"

"She better hope that it will be."

"Mmmmm. Is that your psychological edge...hoping she recognizes a threat?"

"It's a start."

"Let's hope so. Not sure what I can use to dissuade her, but maybe just good scientific logic will work. I feel like a lab rat...spent the last couple of weeks calculating student credit hours and the like."

"Oh. I've got all of that too...and more...and I'm gonna be sure she hears it."

He followed her resolve with the private thought that he could work on Sallie in other ways, ones that satisfied her far more than another victory at the college round-table. Was she really immune to their private life? Surely not. Her posture was likely a ruse, something to keep the college on edge while she pursued some other strategy. Eh? Well, he would find out shortly.

Inside her office, Sallie wiped her lips with her napkin, folding it so her right hand would have access to it at any time.

"Time to get on with it," she muttered aloud, liking the sound of her voice.

She removed her eye and dampened it with *ClearVision*, sanitizing it at the same time. Carefully placed it back in the socket. Flexed her rigid right hand as a gunfighter might preparing for a shoot-out, extended her impaired right leg, adjusted her hearing aid and picked up the phone.

"Send them in, Dottie, please, and take away this coffee."

"Right away."

Zoster turned to the two Chairs, "Dean Drake will see you now." She led them into the office and walked out with the serving tray. With a glance at one another, Emma Burton and David Corrigan ambled across the room.

"Well," Corrigan said, softly, "Here we go."

They scanned the room. Drake sat in her large, supportive chair, neck extending above its leather back, smiling, welcoming them into her space, motioning them with a wave of her hand to the two stiff-backed wooden chairs she had placed in front of her desk. *"Keep them uncomfortable throughout,"* she thought to herself.

"Care for a soft drink, coffee?" she asked, glancing at each of them. "I could ask Dottie to bring in another round, eh?"

"None for me," Corrigan said softly.

"Nope, I'm good," Emma echoed.

They were on edge. Good.

Drake paused, again, softly rubbed the damaged eye socket, leaned forward on her elbows, letting frozen fingers on her right hand dangle outside the line of her device as might a lobster, moving the claw slowly, in time with the motion of her hand which she slid slightly back and forth across the desk. She let the silence weigh a bit more, then spoke, softly.

"I think you both know what I want to explore with you. As I said a few weeks ago in the Chair's meeting, the college is going to have to make some staffing changes to fortify our offerings in Chemistry and Physics."

"Nonsense," Emma replied.

Sallie spat right back, "What did you say?"

"Well, I said, 'nonsense', but I could as easily have said, 'bullshit'."

Drake focused her good eye on Burton, mulled quickly on how to proceed. Frontal assault or mincing step around? She felt a little achy, wondered if she were coming down with something…sniffles…a cold? She re-focused.

"Got something to give me besides dismissal, Emma?"

"You know Sallie, I've been watching you for the past few weeks, trying to get some read on how you see yourself in this new role, waiting to hear something about supporting departments, fighting for faculty, defending programs well established and important to the entire college."

"And…you are not satisfied?" Drake responded.

"For God's sake, no! Look Sallie, I can appreciate your interest in strengthening Physics and Chemistry, but don't be using a regional accreditation report to justify it. I've read that study. It said nothing about requirements for change or a demand for expanded staffing in those departments. It merely read, 'Future department strengthening in Physics and Chemistry may provide additional balance in the science curriculum'."

"That sounds pretty demanding to me," Sallie replied.

"Well, you may be reading it with your bad eye. I hear it saying that as the college expands, it may want to strengthen curriculum in those two areas. Are we expanding?"

"We are not…that's why I believe we need to re-allocate."

"So, let's pursue that, Sallie. Re-allocate. You are suggesting that we take Psychology…the department with the largest student enrollment, the most majors and minors…the highest ranked student evaluation data of any department in the college…you are proposing to cut it…to eliminate four positions, to reduce success in favor of what…a bunsen burner or a larger Newton's Cradle, eh?"

"I prefer to think of it as balancing, Emma. The college can't let all its resources become invested in a bevy of students who don't know why they're here or where they're going. Most of 'em select a curriculum guaranteed to let them study what they seem to care about most...themselves. But our curriculum is not a stand-in for therapy sessions. Where do these people think their futures lie? Eh? They don't know now, and they can take a dozen courses without learning any answers. Just get out in the world and figure it out, eh? Time is their best informant...maybe their late 20s or maybe mid-40s, maybe never, eh?"

"There's a reason for that, Sallie."

"What is it...you really have a reason? Isn't it just the way of the world?"

"Well, that might be, but psychology can help you answer the question of why identity formation occurs as late as it does, why it's the phenomenon it appears to be. Want the answer?"

"No. I'm just making a reference. Psychology majors are overly preoccupied with themselves...should learn more about the world outside of themselves...the physical/chemical world in which we live."

"That would be Blathering 101, eh Sallie? Let's get to the nut of the matter. How will you justify taking four positions that will average 250 students a semester and invest them in a department that will average 12-20 students over the same time period? Is that efficient use of resources? Eh?"

"It's a way of diversifying," Drake answered. "We need to strengthen the sciences."

Emma looked at Corrigan. Was he going to just sit there and be a bump. He needed to jump in here. He caught her look and turned gently toward the Dean.

"Nothing wrong with our segment of the college, Sallie," Corrigan spoke up, "The sciences meet every accrediting standard offered in the past decade. We have great success in Biology, keeping our faculty active and intellectually engaged. Really no different for Chem and Physics. There just isn't as much student interest there. Not our fault. Biology is a very attractive major. Got a dozen students graduating this year. We've sent eight of them on to medical school in the last decade."

"That may be true," she avoided looking at Corrigan directly, but referenced him with a shrug of her shoulder, "but we can balance the sciences better with a few position moves."

"That's pretty much bullshit."

"David Corrigan! You are way out of line right now."

"Well, Sallie, here's a new thought for you. Listen carefully. We aren't giving you any positions. We have a fully tenured department, and no one is eliminating any of them for your soft-hearted pleading about Chem and Physics. You're gonna have to look somewhere else."

"Now, that's the phrase I've been looking for," Emma chimed in. "Go look somewhere else."

The room grew quiet. Drake began massaging the numb fingers on her right hand, shifted her position to ease some discomfort on her damaged knee. Her mind began to race with projections of where this repartee was going to end. Nothing good gonna' happen today. Mulled the impasse she seemed to have ignited and noticed that her headache was back. Adjusted her hearing aid. Maybe best to move conversations a bit into the future. Solidify her position with the Chancellor. Hated a lose a fight. Better to finesse her decision with more quietly held moves.

"Now, listen here, you two. I just don't think this kind of dialogue is going to get us to where I want us to be. Why don't we take some time and let this settle a little and we can talk about it again in a week or so, eh?"

Corrigan came right back into the conversation, "I'll take any efforts to reduce Biology staff right to the Dean's Council, even the Faculty Senate. Better hire your lawyers now, Sallie, cause tenure track position cannot just be deleted. The legal fighting over an effort like that will take a couple of years, at least. We can talk it out next week or next month, but my position won't change."

"I'm sure we can reach an accommodation with some more conversation, David."

"You're gonna lose this, Sallie. Go pick another fight somewhere else in the college, Department of Arts and Theatre, maybe. How many students do those emotionally flawed, creative artists instruct each semester? Eh? A better question: how many students are they luring into bed, closets, and private drawing rooms, eh? How many?"

"David Corrigan!" she paused in exasperation. "We're not talking about personal lives…we're talking about curriculum."

"Really, Sallie…really? Let me rephrase. How many of your theatre majors are screwing the models in your art classes…nothing going on over there except sex, corruption, innocents abused and bad acting… and the worst offense is probably the bad acting. Ever think about hiring a real theatre person to run that department? Eh, Sallie?'"

Silence. Sallie thought quickly about this last provocation. What does David know…really? Hmmm. Suzanna? Best to ignore it and focus on enrollment.

"Well, student loads vary throughout the college, and the creative arts require a lot of personal interaction…can't do life drawing with 200 students in a class," Drake responded.

"Can't turn humanists into chemists and physicists, either, Sallie," Emma chipped in.

"David," she paused, focused her look right on him, raised her voice just a tone, "I'm just not satisfied that the current configuration of faculty is best for the college, for its curriculum, or for options in offering our students the best, most efficient path toward their degrees. That's my job. You may not like it. But, it's gonna happen. I'm not destroying departments; I'm not ignoring their usefulness, but

I'm gonna balance student opportunities, and I'd advise you to start sorting through positions you can best lose."

Corrigan took a light breath, looked intently at her and replied, "Not gonna happen, Sal." *He knew that was a mistake, using the short form of her first name. What the hell.*

Ignoring him, she turned her head toward Emma, "And the same goes for you. Sort it out. I want plans on reducing faculty."

Emma stared at her, then softly pursed her lips and sent her a silent kiss, "Plant that on my ass, Sallie. See how it sorts."

Drake flushed, felt herself losing control, caught it and finally waved them away with her left hand. Dismissal. No comment, she just pointed, "Out". They rose, gave her a pair of final, hard looks and quietly turned toward the door.

"Be sure to close it on your way out, you two," she shouted at them. "It may be the last time you have the chance."

Sallie Drake found herself unbearably irritated, a little shooting pain in her temple, both hands shaking, a rolling sense of nausea in her stomach, white anger warming her face. Those little pricks. Who did they think they were, telling *her* how this was going to end. Nonsense. She shook a little. Took a few minutes to settle herself. Asked Dottie to bring some more coffee. Waiting, she limped about her room, slowly reviewing the conversations with Emma and David, gradually creating new strategies.

Dottie knocked, entered quietly, delivered the coffee, nodded softly and backed away. Lots of tension still in the room. Probably gonna take more than coffee to settle her boss. Wished she could offer her a bit of hard liquor. Maybe someday.

Drake sipped. Feeling better. Picked up her phone, Touched the number. It rang three times. Was she there? Please God, please. It rang again and she picked up.

"Thirty minutes...auditorium...hurry...I need you.

THE OLD

It was here. He felt it. Knew it. Been a long time since he had really considered it, and that was a good thing, he thought. But more recently, he began to feel a decline, an introduction to a final act. A month, then another, and it continued…weaknesses, bowel discomfort, some bleeding. Would not complain to family. Not interested in going to doctors. No finessing what he felt in his body. Didn't care much about what was going on. Not gonna' deal with tests, infusions, or the discomforts of waiting, dreading, listening. Not gonna do it. He would remain in his home and deal with things as they emerged. He was dying. How it occurred, what it was, how fast it might proceed… all this he decided that he did not need to know.

Lying here now, family near, anxiety on faces, wondering how long he would be with them, he leaned a little to one side, felt something inside of him shift and relieve some pressure. Breathed a little easier, but a few minutes later, he returned to his back. Easier there. Could see Margo clearly enough, Ed and Gwen too. Thankful they were there. Been a pretty good marriage, children always a pleasure, even in their teens. Hoped he had given them enough love to keep them settled for the years ahead. He coughed, choked a little, cleared his throat, felt the pain creeping back. Pressed his morphine pump, twice. No sense in stringing his mind out to the very end. Could find peace, he thought, in the solemnity of a lighter mind, a shallow breath. Easier now to get from one to the other. Reminded him a bit of those surgeries back in the day...tonsils, appendix, gall bladder. A masked face momentarily blocked a bright light above him. The instruction to count back from 10. He usually got to eight and then things just faded away. Where was he now...dimly alert but feeling his strength ebbing, his body slipping into that rocking motion he found so restful in his fishing boat. Someone else setting the hook today, he thought, and he didn't care.

He coughed again, choked a bit, but it passed, and he took one more glance at the faces above. A light of their own. Was he done? He guessed he was. Weakening now, he tried a small smile, didn't happen. He paused, closing his eyes, now an easy step. Restful. Here I go, he thought and began to count backward from ten.

10...9...8.......7..........

"We love you Ned. We love you." He heard "love you" but as he noted the phrase, he felt suddenly very weak, shades slipped in front of his vision, and he embraced it...didn't worry about a thing.

There was silence. Margo felt him going, saw the color drain from his face, sensed his body still, and said it again, "I love you, Ned," just in case he could still hear.

She stood there in silence for another minute, then another, but gradually her emotions took her. Her children surrounded her with their arms, all three weeping quietly. He was gone. It was over. What were they supposed to feel now? Was he still there, soul hovering, listening, reassuring them somehow? What did that phrase mean, "Was it over?" Her man, their father...no longer with them. Gone. What was over? Life? His, yes, but not theirs. No return to the energy, the life and love they had shared with him. Damn. That hurt...and they let their tears flow, some quietly marking their cheeks, some accompanied with a sob or two, forcing fluids down their noses, releasing tensions held in place for nearly two weeks now. Hard to adjust, this transition from hope to resignation.

And still, Margo was unclear. What exactly got ahold of him?

Some kind of respiratory issue attacked him, pneumonia in the end, she supposed, but he had pain in his abdomen, was miserable before they finally administered the morphine. Well, his doctors had been attentive to her and to Ted, always there when needed, directing a series of responses to his decline, looking a little puzzled themselves, she thought, but never a doubt in her mind of the quality of his care. The nurses were extraordinary, comforting, expert in their execution of the doctor's orders.

She spent another few minutes next to his bedside, looking again from time to time, each glance convincing her that he had emptied his body, floated into the ether. Ed and Gwen surrounded her with arms and tears of their own for a few more lingering seconds, then moved back, took another look at their father, and then Ed said softly, "I think we should leave now, Mom. Let the staff take dad away, call for the funeral attendant."

"I guess, Ed. I guess."

She paused a few more seconds, then looked at him, glanced to Gwen including her in her comment. "You know, I'm still so confused about what happened to your father. I've thought about this earlier today and feel better each time I do."

"Thought what, Mom?" Gwen asked.

"I would like an autopsy. I just want to know what it is that attacked him so quickly, so suddenly. I think the hospital can provide an autopsy, or at least order one if we want to pay for it, and I do. Money isn't really going to be a problem."

Ed looked at his mother. It wasn't despair talking. She just wanted an answer. Something to settle her, a knowledge that she could take with her into the future.

"Mom, if that's what you want, that's fine with us," he looked at Gwen, she nodded. "Want me to speak to the hospitalist about making those arrangements?"

"Yes, hon. Would you? I'd just feel a lot better. We can take a few days making funeral arrangements while we wait for the results. Might even help the doctors who were treating him. They seemed to be a little mystified all through this."

"They did their best, don't you think?"

"Oh, yes, but I think they were working a little blind, not really sure what it was that grabbed ahold of him. I think we would all like to know a little more."

"O.K. Gwen, why don't you take Mom down to the coffee shop and I'll speak to the hospital and see if we can schedule an autopsy right away...o.k. with you?"

"Oh, sure Ted. Come on, Mom, let's go downstairs to the cafeteria and sit a bit."

As they turned to leave, Ted took one more glance at his father. Yep, he was gone, really gone. Nothing in his own life would ever be quite the same now. That hurt.

He went over the past few days in his mind...again. Hearing from his mom, just three days ago that his father was in the hospital, he wondered why this happened so suddenly. No accident, she said. He had just been not feeling all that good. Didn't want to go to the doctors. Thought he would feel better in a few days.

"How long has it been since he saw his doctors," Ed asked.

"Oh, I don't know. He doesn't like them...in general...you remember how he is...that cracked bone in his leg a decade ago, and he kept walking on it, till it healed...a little gimpy on it afterward... but still, you know...not going to let medical people have a look."

"Has he been feeling bad lately...staying at home...walking much?"

"Pretty much same as always, hon. A bout or two of diarrhea. He cut back his walking every other day about a month ago, then didn't

feel like it at all. Lately seemed to lose interest in much of anything...
but still, no doctors."

"So, what finally got him in here?"

"Pain in his gut...figured it was just some diverticulitis...went on
Flagl for a week, but this time it didn't get better."

"What, he just decided that the pain was too much?"

"I think so, but the loss of energy was pretty discouraging too...
think he figured he had some kind of flu bug or something."

"Well, they admitted him to hospital right away. They must have
seen something?"

"Just told me that they believed he was very sick, drew lots of
fluids, labs and stuff, worked up a profile on MRI and later a PET
scan. First thing they told me was his red blood count was low, and
infection in his colon was real...seemed to be a mass there...not
getting much in the way of benefit from antibiotics ...were going to
do some more work...and then...and then, he just went downhills.
Quietly, but so quickly."

"So, guess it could have been a colon cancer...maybe he was
leaking blood and that caused his weakness?"

"Oh, oh, I guess...I just don't know, Ed. I'd like to."

"I'll see to it, Mom."

"Thank you, hon. Gwen can take me home. I'm exhausted...just
exhausted."

"O.K., I'll be home in an hour or so. Get some quiet time, Mom."

"I will hon."

She turned toward Gwen who had been listening closely to their
conversation. Weeping, she gave her mom a hug, "Let's get out of
here."

****

Derek looked across the table, reminded Andrea that she had a bit of ice-cream on her lower lip, laughed lightly at the way she held a napkin to blot it away. She was both tidy and precise. Not a problem for him, considering that his professional life demanded both.

"Ever consider that a light lunch could segue to a full supper, eh?" he smiled.

"Well, if you're pitching an evening at Toppers, I'm accepting. That'll leave the kitchen lonely for more than 24 hours I think…a habit?"

"Could be. How much fun do ya' have with our pots and pans anyway?"

"Oh, enough to get our food in good portions and on the table, but truth…as you well know Derek…I'm a curious, not a passionate, cook."

"You've been doing it for years…always seems to be enjoying it."

"I've been sitting on the pot for years too. How much do I enjoy that?" she laughed. "One does one's duty."

"I'm making a note to self. More time away from kitchen. Use someone else's toilet. Is that it?" he laughed.

She made an up-and-down motion with her hands, balancing one with the other, smiled. "You gonna order some dessert?"

"I did. Three scoops of French Vanilla. How's that for scintillating sweets, eh?"

"I'll have raspberry cheesecake and a side of cognac."

"Mid-day surprise, eh?"

"I'm gonna enjoy every bit of it…just let it cool my tongue, slide down my throat and keep me alert and happy for whatever we find to do this evening."

"Order one for me too," he smiled.

"Just letting it pile on," she laughed.

"Sweet liquids keep vital organs well lubricated."

"How exactly does that work, Derek?"

"I will show you more about that this evening," he laughed and his eyes sparkled.

Thirty minutes later, they had sorted the preliminaries for the evening, consumed their icy treats, warmed their palates with cognac and said their light goodbyes. She called Uber. He took a message again from the Coroner. "Want this new autopsy finished today, right, Derek"?

"Right," he said to himself. Caught his own ride and in less than 30 minutes, he was in the lab swathed in white, masked, gloved, ready to take the sheet off an older, white man who had died earlier that morning following some complications focused on gut irritation, maybe a blockage, maybe a tumor there. Blood work not flattering. No alcohol, no drugs, but very low RBC count. Bleeding out?

Family requested a look at cause of death. No hysteria about anything, just curious about it. Well, so was he. Always. What precisely had transported this man from a functioning biological agent into a memory for those who survived him? The family would take some comfort just knowing...knowledge cued acceptance. Peace became the by-product of the violent struggles that must have gone on within his body, be it blood loss, tumor challenges or perhaps just a rampant infection in which bugs found a niche and refused to leave...just sent out their scouts and colonized.

Well, it may not be a complicated assessment, Derek thought. Worked his way over the skin, took a good look at the eyes, nothing notable considering that this was a death figure he was looking over. Made the Y incision, and began an inspection of the internal organs...lungs a little spotted, gall bladder gone, liver enlarged but not significantly, heart appeared to be normal size, no evidence of starved tissue.

He moved on down to the colon and saw evidence of bleeding, an eruption of the outer wall which was going to send poisons throughout his body. Yet, the breech was so recent, and so small, it was an unlikely cause of death.

Decided to take a look at one of the coronary arteries. Made an incision, glanced at the interior and lengthened the cut...about 6 inches would do...would tell him whether what he now believed to be true was accurate.

He gently separated the vessel, stretching its two sides back so he had a good look at the interior. Within the artery he found white noodle-like strings, a kind of pulp. He knew them for what they were: white blood cells, blastomas...so plentiful they had piled themselves into spaghetti-like strings, clogging the artery...and where were the red cells, the blood? Not much there, and he had his cause of death: *Acute myeloid leukemia.* Must have struggled with it for a long time, ignoring some of the signs of weakness, but the disease had caused his blood to lose RBC in such amounts that it was just a matter of time... and the time had come. Hoped that helped the family. Even an early diagnosis would have simply taken him down a long exhausting road with slender promises for recovery. Well, he paused...so it goes.

He sewed the chest back together, draped the body and carefully shed his lab garb and gloves. Took a quick shower and exited with some spring in his step. Time to get home to Andrea...a date night out and another serving of dessert.

He smiled

BACK IN THE DAY

Emma Burton stalked back to her office, cursing loudly enough three different students paused and stared at her. "Curious" they thought, and moved on. For her part, she was shaken to her heels. She had played her role in front of the dean, and "Miss Bitch Sallie One-Eyed Drake" had not given an inch, and she could see that the Dean had her good eye on probationary positions in Psychology. They were there all right, Emma thought, and they were productive, talented faces whose skill and insight resonated with students. She was not going to lose them, and most of all, she felt this within her gut, Sallie Drake was not going to win. She would not!

Emma let her mind wander, considering different strategies, comfortable enough with the tools of university dialogue and diatribe. She could hold her own there…and more. But she needed something to keep Drake in her place and out of her department's future. What did she know about her…really? She had been in the history department for several years before wining her position as Dean. What about before? Where had she come from? Did she have a history? Hell, Emma said to herself, everyone does. I'm gonna learn some more about hers.

Where to start? Went to her office, Googled "Dean Sallie Drake" and clicked on *Wikipedia*. Nice account of her life here at Middleton College, with flattering references to her teaching and her new administrative success. "Probably wrote it herself," Emma thought. But what about *before* Middleton. Just some reference to a small college on the plains and according to the write-up, not far from where Drake's parents served as missionaries to Lakota Indians. Well, that was a reach, North Dakota plains to Twin Cities private college. Quite a leap.

Emma became intrigued. Took her nearly half an hour to finally track down Drake's connection to North Plains State College. Hmmm. She went to lunch by herself, and returned in a mood to dig deeper. Looked through the faculty listings for NP State and found a name she recalled from graduate school, Vern Drummond. Lucky? Maybe. What could she remember about him? An irritating face, she thought, but a quiet voice and nicely balanced intellect. That was all. Maybe it was enough. Called the department secretary who rang her through.

"Hello, this is Drummond." Emma heard that voice and remembered his face more accurately...unbroken eyebrows, fluffy cheeks flecked with bad skin, often sunburned. But she also remembered intelligent blue eyes and a disarming intellect which could sort through psych theories and lab data as fast as he could relay a juicy bit of scandal. "He'll know gossip," Emma thought, "Will he spill it?"

"Vern! This is Emma Burton, out here in Middleton College, Twin Cities area, how ya doin'?"

A quiet few seconds passed, then, "Emma! My God this is a treat, twenty years out of graduate school, teaching out here in a lost land and what do I find at the end of my phone, a voice from my past... and one I like."

"Yeah, Vern, I'm out of your past all right, and I have nothing but apologies to send your way for lack of contact. Lives get busy, things change I guess."

"Oh, yeah, Emma, I echo that, and it leads me to a question. What brings you calling?"

"Well, it may be a bit gossipy, but more surely it's a little professional protection on my part, Vern. I'm having a hell of a time with our new Dean here who wants to decimate my department in favor of one of her flavor of the month ideas. I'm gonna fight her every way I know, but, I said to myself, it's always good to have information about someone's past. Has to be something in her career she doesn't want to drag along with her, eh? So I thought I'd ask if you have any insight into her, Sallie Drake."

The connection went silent for a few seconds, and Emma asked, "Vern, you still there?"

"Yep."

"Did you hear me o.k?"

"Yep."

"And?"

"Let me think just a bit…Emma…just a bit."

"Take it away…a few days or a few minutes?"

"A few minutes. Let me call you back."

"Good enough. I'll wait. Thanks, Vern."

"No problem…just give me a few minutes."

Emma touched "OFF", sat back in her chair and began to think. *That was unexpected. What set Vern aback so strongly? Did he know something really delicious, or was he just pondering ethical standards for gossip. We're there any? Hmmm.*

She sorted through various possibilities, hoping for a scandal of financial mismanagement, expecting to hear that Dean Sallie Drake was fired once for poor teaching, assaulting a student, maybe even fighting a tenure decision. Had about decided to head for the gym and some light running, when Vern called back.

"Not sure really if this is what you are looking for, Emma, but stop me at any time."

"Oh, sure," she replied, "Just anything you know."

A pause, again, perhaps for 5 seconds, then Vern began, "Well,

Emma, I don't know much about Sallie Drake, but I know a lot about the person Sallie Drake once was."

"What? She once was nice and now she's a bitch?"

"Well, no. She once was a prick, and she <u>became</u> a bitch."

"Psychological breakdown? Eh? Or did she suffer from some dramatic love affair gone wrong?

"No, no. None of that," Vern said, "I mean it almost literally... prick to bitch. She took a year's sabbatical to start the changes, then she showed up again, a woman so to speak, seemingly full of hormones and an irritable personality. She's a tranny, probably a good ten to twelve years now. How long's she been at Middleton?"

Emma could barely restrain her glee, but she did. "Well, Vern, I think about 8 years...over in history for most of it, got tenure there and then went looking to get into administration. Now, she is our dean. Well, should I say that he is our dean? Or is it 'it'?"

"I always think of 'it' as a useful pronoun compromise between bitch and switch," Vern chuckled, "I'm taken with the 'i' 't' letters in the middle of both words."

"Yeah, well I shouldn't say this, and I know better, but damn, Vern, this is great news...I am so happy she has found her true nature and transitioned into a more comfortable body...yadda, yadda, yadda... you know, but I'm even more pleased to hear what she doesn't want anyone here to know. Have you had any contact with her over the last few years? Just curious?"

"I have not. He...I guess I should say, she... had pretty well completed departure from her earlier identity, and we were getting well adjusted to the short, feminine hair cut, new skirts and short heels, though I gotta say his sense of fashion appeared to be something picked up on an Indian reservation. He had a great boob job, though. But clothing always seemed to be something he fought to get right. Too masculine I thought, but then again, look at her history."

Emma paused in the conversation, digested some of what she was hearing, then asked a question she knew might give her leverage with Sallie Drake.

"Vern, just out of curiosity, what was her manly name when she was there?"

"Ummm, it was Chuck, well she, no he, well guess 'it' at the time, preferred to be called Charles. It's last name was Garland, I think... yep, that was it: Charles Garland. Quiet prick...occasionally caught ignoring rules when under pressure. Pain in the ass as a guy, difficult to connect with him."

"So you knew him before he became a woman, so to speak?"

"Oh, yes. I gotta say, her personality did undergo a substantial makeover. Chuckie had always been a bit of a slime, nothing overtly aggressive, but his new personna occasionally just exploded with anger over academic issues. Ol' Chuck lost a pair, and Sallie Drake found them, and used them, but not often. Probably hormonal imbalances. Has to be tricky keeping a body female...hell has to be difficult *being* female. Anyway, to my eye, she developed a lot more skill in dealing with people than Chuckie had, though she became more reclusive, more reserved. Don't know of any real relationships she developed though there were plenty of rumors about her sex life, as you can well imagine."

"So, this Charles Garland...married?"

"No, and his new persona, sweet little Sallie Drake, wasn't either. At least one guy I remember, who didn't know of her transition, found himself tied in knots, literally, so the rumors went. She was the object of great gossip and we all enjoyed speculating about her private life, and her surgical transformations. I'm not even sure myself what all they do with a penis and where they find a vagina, but however they did it, she seemed comfortable...maybe a good program of hormonal injections. Poke and stick, then poke and sigh, eh? Linguists have a lot of fun with all of this. They know better, but the identification options just trill off their lips in little private conversations. It was probably a good thing that he/she/it found another job."

"So, she just found her moment and left, eh?"

"Yeah, well I think she took up with a Mexican woman, Ida Paszover, and tried to make Cinqo de Mayo into a community holiday. Kind of a north of the border celebration. But it all rang hollow up here. Ida left for California, I think, and Sallie left not long after. We forgot about her, but you bring back some good gossipy memories."

"Well, right now I'm wishing she had landed somewhere else. But, you've been really helpful Vern. Just useful information. By-the-by, if you ever have need of any info from staff out our way, give me a call. I'll let you know how things turn out here. Should be over in a couple of months I would think."

"Sounds just fine, Emma. Enjoyed the chatter and some of the memory recall for sure. Watch out for this Dean Sallie whatever she calls herself. I still think of her, rather of him, as good old Chuckie Garland, a stuffed snot in his own way, and a vindictive one. If she's in a powerful position, you'll feel the heat, for sure. Just a jerk. Well, again, enough about him, well her. Take care, Emma. Stay in touch."

"I will, Vern. I will."

DOTTIE'S DISCOVERY

She lay in her own bed, clothed in silky pajamas, surrounded with mixed scents and a sense of peace she had been seeking for days. The still-edgy memories of her afternoon in the auditorium along with another evening with Suzanna helped shed her frustrations with Emma and David. Wasn't gonna call him at all 'til this whole mess was over. She had overestimated his weakness for her...happened sometimes with guys. But he'd be back. Didn't much care what the university knew about her affair with David. Let them guess. Food for gossip, but nothing to compromise her work. Normal enough.

Her activity with Suzanna was a little more risky, though they could pal around in public. Women shopped together, had lunch together, went to theatre together and no one looked twice. She wanted to improve her fashion to reflect her new status in the university and Suzanna knew clothes, along with drama and art. Best of all, she thought, Suzanna knew *her* wants and catered to them.

But her "auditorium tryst" was something else. There could be no defense or sympathy for it by administration, faculty or students. The general public would clamor so loudly she'd lose her job. Yet, weird as it seemed to her, the darkness of the projection booth let her feel more free, more unleashed than any of her other intimate unions. In that secluded exchange of whispers, she became convinced she was loved in an intimacy that permeated her entire being. That voice did not instruct her, correct her or try to reshape her. It respected her, absorbed her. In that dark, recessed void, she found herself unbound, and unwound. She shook her head in bewilderment. Didn't Willie Nelson have a song about making hard choices? She thought a bit, ran one of the lines through her head, something about why she had to choose...make everybody lose. Willie's right. She didn't have to change a thing.

She peeled back the covers, lubricated and inserted her dildo expander, waited some time to get the daily effect, then walked into a pre-warmed shower. Gave passing thought to a wish that a penis could keep her vagina in good form, but none could...at least none she had found. Removed the expander, soaped and shampooed body and hair. Dried. Dressed. Finished makeup. Injected her daily dose of hormones and walked through a spray of Camellia perfume Suzanna had bought her. Felt a bit of a headache trying to take form and found her body a little achy. No day for any of that. Swallowed her last bit of coffee with two NSAIDs and left for the college. Another department meeting today, and she was ready to finish it up. They'd be trying for more delay, but there would be none. Time to act. She shivered just a bit, anticipating the look on their faces when she closed down their protests and laid down the law. Power. Delightful.

She parked, noted that she was getting better at maneuvering her knee brace and got to the door in a record ten minutes. As she turned to the last corridor that led to her office, she saw Corrigan coming up alongside her. For just a moment, she lost her resolve, reached out and simply touched his hand as he passed. He smiled, even as he gently pushed back against it. Neither looked at one another.

But someone was looking. Dottie Zoster turned out from the ladies restroom heading back to the office and noticed that touch... the slight reach of the Dean's hand, Corrigan's response and the light scent of Camillia in the trailing air.

Oh, my…what was that? Holding hands…well…touching hands… and a new perfume on the Dean? Eh?

She knew all the gossip about Dean Drake's love life, and she occasionally took a close look at her appointments, but she saw nothing in her schedules, nor her memory, indicating Corrigan, or anyone else, had some special status. She took a deep breath and stopped to kill some time while the Dean made it back to the office. She would check her records more closely.

As Sallie walked into her office, she felt her knee give way a bit, lurched a little getting into her chair, took a deep breath and called out to Dottie for some coffee.

"She's out right now," Doris said, should be right back.

As if on cue, Dottie appeared, saw the look and called out, "Coffee on the way."

"Bring me some of your eyeball moistener, too, Dottie. This thing is killing me."

"Right away."

Drake sat down in her chair, letting out a small "ooomph" as the bad knee gave out just as her bottom met the back of the seat. *Maybe that was why her back had been aching lately, she murmured to herself.* The chair rocked a bit, settled. She swung it around to give herself the view she loved to visit: the college interior park and walkways hosting student movement and sometimes grassy picnics and chat groups. *Wonderful campus, she thought. Now if her damn eye would quit hurting, she could look forward to seeing Burton and Corrigan. Those names…Burton and Corrigan…a vaudeville act? She grinned.*

A few minutes later, Dottie appeared in the doorway with a tray bearing hot, dark roast coffee, cream and sugar, and a small vial of liquid for the Dean's bad eye.

"I want you to try this new eye solution, Dean Drake. I'll leave you to open it as you prefer. Made in India. It may to be more effective than *ClearVision.*" She looked at the label again…"*ClearBo: Safe and provides a more slippery surface for the acrylic eye.*" She surveyed the room, noted how weary Drake looked…probably a bad night worrying about this morning's meeting with the Chairs.

When Sallie didn't swing around immediately, Dottie just took her cue and sat the tray on the desk, urged her to relax a little before meeting the chairs, and left. Returning to her desk, she took some time to look over the Dean's appointments for the past three months. Found seven names that had some regular appearances: David Corrigan, Chair of Biology, Adam Crossover, Chair of Political Science, Eleanor Rouse, Chair of English, Trevor Coxswain, Chair of Chemistry, Suzanna Ludlow, Chair of Arts, Theatre, Emma Burton, Chair of Psychology, and Gerald Sackmaster, Chair of Physics.

Well, all this chatter about curriculum change and staffing shifts probably brought them in to plead their cases. Burton and Corrigan's faces were always focused and intense when they showed up and the conversations were sometimes a bit noisy. Coxswain simply slid in and out. Said nothing. Very quiet fellow. Rouse usually just needed a pep talk…how could someone so disorganized run a department, Dottie wondered? Ludlow spent more time in there than the others, but the topic was theatre staffing, and Dottie enjoyed listening to the chatter. Drama, romance, comedy and stage were topics she understood. Did not remember anything unusually personal ever said between the two, though Suzanna always left a perfume lingering in the still air. And she thought…jumped a little. The scent in the hallway trailing the Dean was the same as she remembered from Suzanna's last office visit. So when did the Dean pick up the perfume…a gift?

Dottie reflected some more, sorting through her views until she finally settled on a conclusion. Dean Drake was simply maneuvering to political purpose, stroking egos, building quiet relationships. Getting ready for an academic confrontation. Curriculum and personnel changes remained a constant source of commentary in and out of the office. Maybe Corrigan and the Dean were covert allies. There had been talk about creating an Assistant Dean position. He might have his eye on that and would accept reorganization for a promotion, despite his vocal objections. Or…maybe Suzanna had an ambition to work beside Dean Drake.

But…she asked herself a new question. All this fighting! Why? Why would Dean Drake go looking for a huge struggle with established departments when she was only a few months on the job? Ambition was part of her DNA, but weren't there other ways of pursuing it? And now, Corrigan, touching hands with her. What was that all about? A betrayal of his verbal objections to personnel changes? Anything going on there…or with Emma Burton? And that perfume link to Suzanna Ludlow? Would her Dean mix sex and curriculum and call it college improvement? It wouldn't be the first time a woman had used sex to persuade men to bond to her, but her own history told her that usually backfired with jealousy and ambition.

And change…in department staffing? Even she, Dottie Zoster, knew nothing disturbed faculty more than change, and Sallie embodied change. Was she using some kind of physical relationship to smooth personnel reassignments. If so, how much…and with whom? When she saw him just now, where was Corrigan going anyway? Was Dean Drake launching her new career with sex? Dottie had a hard time believing that. But where was Corrigan now?

She could have found him outside, walking across the Quad alongside Emma Burton, planning a meeting strategy. "David, I think I have something that could give us real leverage, assuming you're ready to go to the wall on this faculty reassignment issue."

He stopped his walk.

"I am. No reason to hold back at all. Sallie's ideas'll ruin my department whatever benefits it brings to Chem and Physics. Whaddya' got?"

Emma began describing what she had learned from her sources in North Dakota and as she did, Corrigan paused walking and just stared at her.

His stomach turned as he sorted through the mixed message Emma gave him. How had he never discovered what he now knew to be true. Sallie Drake, transgender. Sallie Drake, his lover. Sallie Drake, so active in bed yet so cautious about being touched between her legs. A home for his penis but a barrier to his fingers. He began to feel sick to his stomach. Christ, that surgery must have been pretty tricky. Castration to begin, then slice open a space in the pudenum, insert erectile tissue from the penis creating the walls of a vagina, and use part of the penile head for a clitoris. Insert a dildo to stretch and hold the new pocket. Shorten the ureter. All that to welcome his own little buddy into the warm, moist, active shelter that Sallie Drake created for him…and others. Formed quite a haven for his penis-into-penis assault down there. Had to be scar tissue no doubt. He grimaced. Maybe those were the little lumps that he sometimes brushed across, wondering what injury she might have suffered. That now made sense, and it humiliated him as much as her curriculum plans enraged him.

He and Emma continued walking, talking, gesturing, halting, planning. A half hour earlier, he had touched Sallie's hand as they passed in the hall. Now he felt the need to scrub it spotless. Told Emma he would meet her at the meeting and drifted off to the men's rest room. Cleansed his hands once, then again. Dried them thoroughly, tried to zipper his new perception into its own little emotional pocket and walked down to the meeting. As he approached the door, Sallie, standing at her place, glanced over, welcomed him in with a smile. He couldn't return it.

Curriculum is never a joking matter, she thought. He'll feel better tomorrow night. She had plans for him.

She struggled a bit to sit without Corrigan's assistance, then turned to the chairs, drew a breath and began.

"As I indicated a few weeks ago, I'm going to move faculty from Psychology and Biology over to Chemistry and Physics. Now, of course, what that really means is that two departments will be losing some teaching faculty and two departments will be hiring new expertise. This is painful I know. Two tenured Biology faculty will be leaving us, and losing four probationary appointments in Psychology is going to be noticed, but it's for the good for the college…and for the university."

She smiled.

"I have talked to the chairs of all four departments and while it's certainly natural for Emma and David to resist these losses, I think I have made it clear that there will be no delay. Losing some faculty will coincide with the hiring of others and by next fall, we should be offering a greatly strengthened curriculum in the sciences."

She paused.

"Any questions? David, Emma?"

"Nothing from me," Corrigan answered.

"I'm still digesting things for the moment, so no," Emma murmured.

"Well, that makes for a short meeting," Sallie looked surprised. She addressed the entire group once more, "Don't forget to submit those uniform department rules before the end of the month. Don't know how you all operated with the mish-mash that I have been looking through. In a year's time, we'll be more efficient, more effective and more resilient in providing curriculum for our students…and isn't that what it's all about…our students."

The chair of Physics, Gerald Sackmaster, commented, "You bet, Dean...always need to think about the students."

Eleanor Rouse echoed the remark, "Whatever the size of classes, we have to teach our students and this move is an improvement, and we may need to improve our social support for them...bathrooms need to be well-equipped."

As often occurred, Rouse's last remark left the group speechless.

Corrigan and Burton said nothing.

Outside, in the hall, they spoke briefly to one another. "Let's meet with her tomorrow morning, David, and let her know what we have."

"Yep," Corrigan smiled.

"Done," Emma smiled. "See you later."

"Looking forward. Let's put an end to her."

LEVERAGE

Sallie gathered herself, took a deep breath and tried to relax. She moved her swivel chair left and right, found focus on the empty space out in the quad, filled now with small groups of students, perhaps 3-4 in a bunch. She reached forward and opened one of the small windows so she could hear a bit of the talk. Mid-day chatter, some studying, even a little laughter moving their bodies. She found some solace in that. At least someone was happy. Suddenly, a topic emerged that caught her attention. She moved a bit to get her good ear focused on the chatter below.

"Guess what, Aime! I'm gonna graduate this May…only took me seven years to get out of here," she laughed.

"Oh, my God, Carrie! What in the heck took you so long?"

"Well, I changed majors four times and so, you know, all those new requirements just kept me in school, year after year."

"Four times! Really? Can't imagine that…and so what did you finally settle on?"

"History. It seemed most interesting though I don't know what I'll do with it…not going to teach…not going to graduate school…still…I am gonna get my diploma!"

Sallie had heard enough and closed the window. Students! No accounting for purpose or progress…half the freshman never graduated. Had to be a better way? Who knew? History was interesting but unemployable. She knew that. Students discovered it. Maybe she should take three positions from History and create a Women's Studies Department. Cater to the flavor of the year...or maybe send them to English...but what would Eleanor Rouse do with them? Hard to imagine.

Well, time to get to it. She swung around, pushed up from her desk with her good left arm, protecting the damaged fingers on her right hand. Stood. Adjusted her hearing aid. Gently rubbed that artificial eye that seemed to need more attention lately. Felt good to massage it. Wished she could bring the same comfort to the rest of her body. It hurt, ached really, and that headache visited too often. Fighting with faculty was exhausting.

She moved around the desk

"Dottie...some coffee, please."

"Right away. Don't forget you have appointments with Corrigan and Watson again this morning. They'll be here shortly."

"Oh, yes...how could I forget that," Drake answered with some edge in her voice. "Just send them in. I'm gonna just look out my window and relax a little. My eye is killing me. Something seems to be grinding away in my upper eyelid. I'm kind of achy too...getting a hell of a headache. Can you bring me more of that new cleaner you have?"

"Oh, sure." Dottie answered.

She opened her desk drawer and took out *ClearBo*, walked into the office and offered it to Sallie as she removed the false eyeball and held it in her hand.

"Give it a good go," Dottie commented.

Sallie did, pouring the solution into her palm, rotating the eyeball around in it until it was fully saturated. She brought out two tissues and gently wiped it. Held it up to the light and saw the gleam of clean.

She put the eye back in place, grimaced a bit, then relaxed. Should be easy in the socket. "How's it look, Dottie?"

"Quite secure...don't hesitate to use that *ClearBo* whenever it gets irritated. I'll send in coffee when they show up. O.K.?"

"Oh sure. Thank you, Dottie. I'm gonna rest for a bit. Can you close the door...quietly."

"Consider it done."

She let her arms relax, and set her hands over themselves to keep them in her lap. Closed her eyes, looked into the black and felt it grow stronger and deeper.

"Ahhhhh", she exhaled, and let the air slip out some more.

Corrigan and Burton walked into the office, neither smiling.

"Hi Dottie. Is she in?"

"Oh, yes, David. But she's having a bit of a rough morning, I think. May be napping a little, but coffee's ready. That should perk her up."

"Let us bring it to her. Our duty is to smile and serve, right?"

Dottie laughed, "You are so right, David. I'll mix the milk and sugar for her. Let me send it in with you. Lot easier than dealing with a tray and stuff. She can sip it while you three talk."

"Perfect."

Dottie went over to the J-Cup, pressed some buttons, waited for the mug to fill and tore packages of Sweetener, two as always. Fumbled getting the wrappers into the trash, but fingered them free, added two tablespoons of milk, stirred the cup and turned to Corrigan.

Emma watched Dottie work, growing a little more impatient with every delay. This was jackpot time...and she wanted to get to it... began rehearsing her comments. Oh, the look on Drake's face will be something to remember.

Dottie interrupted, "She's gonna love this...may need to cool a bit...she likes it white and sweet."

"Yes, she does," Corrigan smiled.

He turned, opened the door quietly, and they stepped in. Drake was facing the window, watching open spaces. He sat the coffee mug on her desk. Paused. Listened. Watched.

No sound, then finally, a clearing of the throat and Drake turned around.

"So, you two! What could we possibly have left to say after our last meeting. I'm really a bit surprised in you David. And you, Emma…I saw you as a professional…able to bounce with the ebb and flow of college business. Eh?"

Corrigan took the lead, explaining in general how damaging the reassignment of positions would be to his small department.

"But there's more, Sallie, some complicating information that Emma has stumbled across."

"And what might that be?" Sallie asked with a bit of disdain in her voice. "Just what might that be, eh? Whaddya' have, Emma?"

Emma began in a low tone, describing her friend at NGPC, Vern Drummond, and what she had learned about the general subject of Sallie's faculty development over a few years, particularly that of Chuckie Garland.

"Is that a name you know, Sallie…this guy, Chuckie Garland?"

Silence.

"Do you really want me to have to spell this out for you, Sallie. It's a mess, and you know its gonna be a career killer in a small college like this one."

Silence.

Emma glanced at the dean's face. Saw nothing yet. No problem. There's more to come. She proceeded to report all that she had learned in her conversations with Vern. She offered Sallie rough dates of the surgical timeline and gender change that could now be confirmed by faculty she left a long time ago. Sallie began shifting her body placement, clawing her throat lightly with her bad hand, catching her breath, suppressing pain and confusion. Her face slowly evolved from surprise to skepticism, from embarrassment to fright, to horror.

Emma saw it all and pressed her offer, "Neither David nor I are interested in tossing your private medical issues into the air and letting gossip take them hither and dither," Emma concluded. "And we won't, IF we just have your assurance about postponing these staffing changes for another year...or two...and finding somewhere else to look."

Emma stopped speaking and just stared at the Dean, pinpointing her look so intensely she might have been throwing darts. Sallie's mind just kept spinning. She glanced at Corrigan and her heart sank. Clearly, he was not handling this information with any sense of sophistication.

Corrigan cleared his throat and looked away from her, his thoughts forming quickly, penetrating his emotional cloak and reaching into the darkest part of his heart. Their relationship was over, and he began feeling nauseous as he thought of the intimacies he had shared with her, or was it "it"? The urgency of seduction he now saw as the consumption of the spider by the fly. He knew why she did not liked to be touched between her legs, and he laughed at his memory of a sit-com character who said women had seven erogenous zones. Well, did a tranny have more...or less? Sure, he could add it all to a sexual history that he had always enjoyed...adventurous, open-minded, non-judgmental, but this...a transgender something in his bed...no... not ever. But there "she" or rather there "it" was. He could scarcely breathe.

But it was not his reaction that would ruin Sallie Drake, Corrigan thought...no, it would be the judgment of others, and those higher, in the community and throughout the faculty. Students not so much, but others would punish her/it with pleasure, over and over. He could just stand by and watch. Most satisfying of all, the freak would have to concede and give up her plans for reorganization. They had won.

Sallie gathered herself. Took a deep breath, turned away, exhaled. She knew sometime, somewhere, her transgender journey would become known, but it was supposed to be on her terms. Now, on the cusp of a huge academic victory over a recalcitrant college, she confronted the untimely, and uncontrollable release of her most vital personal secret. What could she say to these two, Emma, angry and relentless, Corrigan, a stunned, disappointed lover. What to say? What to do?

She finally cleared her throat, gathered herself, turned and stared at the two of them with her good eye. She spat out the words.

"You two pig fuckers can go screw yourselves!"

As she screamed her defiance, she grimaced so hard, so fully, that her eyeball ejected from her socket and landed on the desk, bounced twice, rolled slowly to the center, stopped and settled.

"Her desk must be perfectly level," Corrigan thought.

Dottie heard the scream and jerked alert in her chair. No closed door, could contain that rage. She pretended to arrange some things on her desk and moved a little closer to the door. She held her breath, listened to silence, one so pronounced that she grew a little alarmed.

Inside, Sallie Drake squinted hard and glanced at both Corrigan and Watson, then with as much dignity as she could muster, quietly picked up her eyeball, cupped it in her hand and, after a long pause, continued. *"It's a new world! Even if I didn't choose this moment, I'm sure as hell not going to let your fucked up threats affect my professional judgments!"*

"I've always known that when this day came, I would either ascend or self-destruct, and my sense of it all was that if I could control the narrative, I could succeed. I'm gonna have to rethink that…but I can tell the two of you right now, the reorganization is going to happen,

and I am going to go public with it, to faculty and to community alike This week. No delay. No appeal. You can say anything you want to say to the general faculty or the public. So, fuck you Emma! Fuck you, David! Wait, I already have. Fuck you both! Get out of here!"

She motioned them out of the room and concluded the sweep of her arm by deftly placing the acrylic eye back in its socket.

Stunned, Corrigan and Burton sat there, staring at her handling of her eyeball, absorbing the verbal assault, sorting through some possible response. They moved toward the door, and Corrigan opened it slightly, then turned back to Drake. *"Is that what you're gonna tell Suzanna Ludlow, Sallie? 'Get the hell out of here'. You gonna lose another lover, eh? You think I didn't know about that...I just didn't care about Suzanna, so long as you were good in my bed...and you were...but no longer. Transgender! Eh! You! You make me heave."*

Emma looked at Drake, stared at her, held the gaze, finally spoke. *"Sallie. You are a freak."*

Silence. It lengthened. Drake just kept staring at them with her good eye, slowly, repeatedly raking her claw across the center of her desk. Corrigan and Emma exchanged glances, both surprised, alarmed, their flushed faces warming the temperature in the entire room.

Each thought the same, *"We are going to destroy her."*

They nodded in turn to Sallie, said nothing more and walked out, quietly closing the door behind them.

Dottie was stunned. Raised voices were not unusual in the Dean's office, but the intensity of these exchanges, their venomous tones, were unique, and Dottie heard something that alarmed her even more...the Dean's comment, *"I already have..."* reference to having sex with Corrigan. Really? And what of Suzanna Ludlow? Another lover? Followed by Corrigan's comments that Drake was transgender! Transgender...my God! What was going on? Was her own Dean physically re-structured? Was she serving as secretary for a compilation of body parts unknown to her senses? Did that scent of Camellia which floated around the Dean from time to time provide evidence of something more than a heavy spray by Suzanna? Could it?

Dottie's stomach cramped. Moose Lake, her hometown, featured none of this. As a local radio voice once said about it, "Everyone was above average," and she was raised to serve and support her superiors. Honesty remained a core value. No tales of sexual activity ever rested even lightly on her name, and she was a black hole for university gossip. Direct communication, proper attire and polite conversation defined her. She carried a positive outlook, encouraged her staff and maintained the very essence of professionalism. She controlled her only vanity, wrinkles in the corner of her eyes, with periodic botox injections…a very thin needle…a very careful dosage. Indeed, her success with botox sold her on the Dean's new eye lubricant, *ClearBo* and it seemed to have worked. Drake used it more often, and it did provide her relief. But Sallie seemed to be in a different kind of pain now. Her rant to Corrigan and Watson? Could it be? Really? Was she? What was she saying? Unbelievable!

She wasn't feeling well at all. She flushed, stood up and quietly walked out of the reception area, mentioning to her assistant Doris Leveling, that she would be gone for the rest of the day. Upset stomach.

As Dottie walked down the hall to the parking lot, Sallie stepped out of her office looking for her. "She's taking the rest of the day off," Doris said calmly. "Looked like she was coming down with something. Thought she'd be back tomorrow morning."

"Good enough," Sallie replied, "Say Doris, keep my morning open tomorrow. I have some things to think about. Gonna leave early myself. It's been a hell of a day."

"Absolutely, Dean Drake."

Sallie took a deep breath, felt her head beginning to pound, turned and gathered her personal items from the office and headed home. Maybe a good drink, or three, would calm her. Or maybe she should just call, Suzanna. Eh? Her spirits began to rise, and she made it to her car without catching a knee or bumping into a door edge. Yes, Suzanna. Been awhile.

They spent the evening together, chatting, loving, eating, joking, caressing, polishing the bonds they had developed over the past several months. Somewhere between 9 and 10 p.m., Sallie excused herself to go to the bathroom, and as she got up from the sofa, her cellphone fell out of her lounging pajamas. Sallie didn't notice. Suzanna picked it up, carelessly glanced at it to see a pop up text message from David Corrigan? *"Hey, tranny, you gotta' call off this curriculum review. I know about North Dakota. I'll shout you out. You'll be done here!"*

Suzanna stared...and stared. North Dakota? What the hell was that all about? She knew it was part of Sallie's academic history, but "tranny"? What was that supposed to mean...really? *Sallie Drake was transgender*...that's what it meant and Suzanna sat and took a breath...several of them, assessing her emotions, absorbing the physical meaning of what she just learned.

Transgender...did it matter? No.

David Corrigan in Sallie's bed! That's what mattered.

Her gut shrank so suddenly it cramped her breath. Her relationship with Sallie was exclusive...or so she believed...and Corrigan's threat detonated a cascade of bodily ills...light sweat, lumps in her stomach, mental confusion, a kind of blind anger that erupted in her mind and fed her body. She twisted her torso a little in pain, seeing a truth she fought to reject. Could it be true? David Corrigan? And an inner voice told her, *"Of course it could"*. Betrayal was an old story. But...oh my God! Her own story? Surely not? Why not? Eh? What's next? What to say? When? Explanations? A long cramp shot through her belly. One thought...revenge!

A BIG BIG DAY

David Corrigan wandered down the hall, glancing into offices, noting the calm and early morning comforts in the Chancellor's Office, the intensity of conversation in Affirmative Action, even the occasional laughter from Extended Education. Happy people, he thought. Happy in their work. Happy in their lives. He wasn't.

Slowly, he opened the door to the Dean's office, caught Dottie's eye and asked if he could have a minute with Sallie.

"Not sure, David. She was pretty upset with everything that seems to be going on yesterday. I had to talk and settle her down when she first came in. I think she may have an ear infection...dealing with a headache too...really kind of shaky...and that eye...my goodness... she can hardly lubricate it enough. I practically had to empty the bottle into her eye socket this morning. I'm gonna have to order some more. She says the eye may have to be replaced. And...yesterday, she left early...so did I. So give me a minute. Just wait here. Let me have a glance."

Dottie returned. "She seems to be just resting. I'm guessing that it might be fine to see her. Just don't upset her, eh?"

Corrigan smiled wryly, "I can understand that...no, I'm not gonna get into it with her again."

He walked into Sallie's office, saw her in her chair facing the quad, back to him. He cleared his throat lightly, "Say, got a minute, Sal?"

She said nothing. Did not turn.

"Damn," he thought. Maybe her hearing aid was turned off. He looked again and saw it on the desk. She must have taken it out while she was resting. She really is taking this hard. Well, it's a pudding of her own making.

He approached her softly, nearly whispered, "Sallie, hon, can we talk?"

She did not respond. He saw her head resting on her chest, deeply relaxed. Oh, Christ, she was napping. He waited another minute, then left, closing the door and mentioning to Dottie, "She seemed to be sleeping, so I'll just come back. Let 'er know I was here."

"No problem David."

As he walked out the door, Emma Watson approached from down the hall.

"What did she say?"

"Not a word. Napping. Seemed pretty exhausted. Bet this stuff is draining her."

"Well, fuck her. Tired or not, I'm gonna give 'ol Chuckie Garland a little more to think about."

"Have at it," Corrigan smiled and walked away down the hall.

Emma walked in, nodded a hello to Dottie and asked if Sallie were ready to see her.

"I think so, Emma. But not if you wanna make war on her. She's exhausted. She may be nodding off a bit, but she wants to meet with you...maybe let me make her a cup of coffee and you can take it in to her."

"Excellent," Emma waited for Dottie to mix the brew, took in the aroma and noted that she probably needed a cup herself. Walked into the Dean's office and took a sip, white and sweet. Not bad. Took another, left it half full. Good enough, she thought, and gently approached Sallie's desk. Saw her resting in her chair, chin on her chest, in deep sleep. Walked closer quietly with hot, sweet white coffee still steaming in her hand. Set it on the desk, spoke softly, "Dean Drake...you awake? Just resting?"

Did she hear her? Head seemed to move slightly. Clearly tilted just a tad leaving the bad ear to catch sound? Noted the hearing aid on the desk. She tried again, "Dean Drake"?

No answer.

Well, wake her or leave her? Eh? Hard to argue with anyone coming out of a deep doze. She left, mentioning to Dottie that the Dean seemed to be pretty tired, napping, and she'd see her tomorrow. "Left her coffee there...she might awaken fast enough to find it still warm."

"Not a problem, Emma. I'll let her rest awhile, and get her moving in time for her luncheon with the Chancellor."

Time passed. Students came into the office, made appointments. Three other chairs came by, Sackmaster, Physics, who had no interest in speaking to a sleeping Dean. He just shook his head, raised and lowered his shoulders, grimaced and left.

Eleanor Rouse, English walked in next, and she quibbled a bit. "I really need to see her, Dottie. I have growing problems with the amount of paper products in the women's rest room...but I don't want to wake her. Could you? Maybe I could have a minute?"

"Not now, Eleanor, not for that. I'll report to her and she'll get back to you, eh?"

"I guess so...but let her know, please Dottie, that the situation is just intolerable. I even have students complaining to me and I just don't know what to do. Paper products are key to stability you know."

"I'll do it, Eleanor," Dottie smiled to herself, turning to look at the next face in the entry...Suzanna Ludlow, Art/Theatre. Gave her the same story. Dean was resting for awhile.

Ludlow pressed the issue slightly.

"Could I just take a peek and see if she is stirring? She wanted to discuss a private issue with me."

"Oh, Suzanna," Dottie frowned. "You know, she's been so tired of late, I really hate to disturb her. These little naps she takes really revive her."

"Well, yeah. Maybe just a peek in to see if she is stirring?"

"Well, just a quiet one, eh."

Ludlow went to the door. Opened it, stepped inside and approached her lover. She could see Drake dozing. She walked quietly closer, reached the edge of the desk. "Say darlin'," she began, "I'm sure happy you came over last night. Like to talk a bit about phone messages."

No answer, and Suzanna decided not awaken her...maybe just leave a little token on the desk. She took out a white acrylic flower set on a ring, a tiny Camellia as Sallie had requested. She walked quietly up to the desk, thought she saw Sallie move just a bit, waited. No awakening. She moved the hearing aid aside and placed the ring where it would be sure to be seen, paused then spoke softly to Sallie, "Loved our time together last night...come again...and soon." No response. She swallowed her disappointment in not being able to confront her about David Corrigan. But not now. Quietly turned and left.

"Be sure to tell her I came by, Dottie. Will visit again maybe tomorrow, eh?"

"Oh, sure, Suzanna. She'll look forward to it." As she commented, Dottie felt herself squirming...what was it that Suzanna was mumbling in there...something about last night and coming again? Double *entendre* chatter in the Art/Theatre Department was common enough, but this seemed personal...far too personal...and she caught herself imagining again what Corrigan had suggested about Ludlow the day before...a lover to the Dean, as was he himself. And then, that shattering comment about the Dean being transgender? Possible? She shook her head slightly, in confusion. No. Not possible. She would have known.

Twenty minutes passed, and Dottie decided nap time was over. She went into the office, speaking as she advanced to Sallie's desk. "O.K., Dean Drake, I think it's time for you to get ready for the luncheon, eh?"

Drake was still facing the commons, head still resting on her chest, tilted left. Dottie moved around the desk slowly, not wanting to startle her. Saw one eye closed, the bad one slightly open. Sallie must be in a deep sleep, she thought. Her coffee cup was still full, so she hadn't been sipping. Bad ear without its aid, but full of what looked like ear wax. *"How did that happen? She needs to clean it more often."* Dottie reached out and nudged Sallie's shoulder to rock her awake. One gentle push and nothing. Two touches and a growing panicky concern. She took a sharp look at Sallie's face. Drained, pale, her bad right eye staring. Dottie looked closely at her chest, glanced at her face again. Colorless cheeks. She wasn't breathing, or was she? Checked her chest for respiration. Nothing. Not breathing at all!

"Oh my God. OH MY GOD!"

Dottie rushed to her desk, grabbed the phone and dialed 9-1-1 as she shouted to the office, "SHE'S DEAD! THE DEAN IS DEAD!"

CHESTER DEVLIN

He'd been around a while. If you asked some of the youngsters, maybe he'd been around too long. Nearly 10 years now since he had become Chief of Detectives, District 8, which included Woodland Park. He had a fond spot for that little community, given his work with local puzzle solver, Jonas Kirk, and more than a decade of dealing with occasional homicides. While crime rates didn't seem to get any smaller, even his critics had to admit Devlin had a way of finding the truth on big cases...or maybe stumbling upon it...but he owned his work whatever it might produce: success or failure. Asked about arrest rates, he might mumble something about people everywhere were good, just sometimes got themselves into bad situations. Some of his critics might say, "What then? Are you fighting crime, Chester, or sympathizing with killers while moping up the messy remains of murder? Pasting flyers of bank robbers around the widows of local business shops doesn't count as police work, does it, Chester?"

That was when Devlin would stop talking, retreat into his office, phone a buddy or call his wife, Geraldine. Friends would remind him that he had been working the local crime scene more than two decades and always to general success. There was a reason he had been promoted to lead District 8. They might point out the numerous ways the local *Gazette* sang his praises, and no one could forget the way he solved what were called the *"Marquis Murders"*. Some still wanted him to go to Polynesia and arrest the killer. But without an extradition agreement, Devlin knew it would be a flight too far. He preferred to focus his time where it could be more productive.

When the 9-1-1 call came through that Wednesday, he responded with energy, commitment and a certain nostalgia. Had been quite a while since an unexplained death had brought him into contact with the community or the coroner. Seemingly benign, the alert merely stated that the Dean of the College of Arts, Letters and Science, Dr. Sallie Drake, over at Middleton College, had been found dead in her office. Medics had been called, but she was cold and they didn't disturb the body. It appeared she had suffered a heart attack, but there were some surrounding dynamics that led the local coroner both to pronounce her dead and to alert Devlin to the possibility of homicide.

"Chester, I think I want you to come over here and take a look at the scene before I go about moving the body," Coroner William White commented to him on the phone.

"Why? Whadya got?" Devlin replied.

"I got people who think someone killed her. What do I do with that?"

Silence.

"O.K., Bill, I hear ya. I'll be over directly to take a look. Ya think this is gonna require an autopsy?"

"Oh, I would think so. Sudden, unexplained death. Got to have an answer to that."

"I'll be right over...take me maybe 15-20 minutes."

"Good. My estimate is that she has been dead for a few hours now. Microbes working, you know...time to get her into refrigeration."

"I'll hurry."

White heard the phone disconnect. He had Devlin's attention and the process of examining a sudden death to the satisfaction of both police and medical examiner had begun. He gave thought to the next step after removal...autopsy...and decided that he would direct the body to Dr. Derek Jackson. Experienced and cool under pressure, Jackson would give him exactly what he wanted: scientific explanation of a sudden death. Nothing in the general community was going to influence his findings and, above all, White wanted an unequivocal judgement.

Pocketing his cellphone, White looked around the office from where he was calling Devlin, and counted faces: a secretary, Dottie something, and her assistant, Doris. Both seemed to think that Sallie Drake had been murdered. Four hourly workers, none of whom were around that morning before the Dean died, had no opinions about anything. Had to be more traffic and for that White would need records, conversations, memories, maybe even video footage if there were any security cameras. Well, a mess, but in just a few minutes, the scene here would be Devlin's and Sallie Drake would be off to the cooler where she could await the fine hand, scalpel, needles and saw of Derek Jackson.

White tapped his foot impatiently. Almost 20 minutes gone, gonna remind Devlin there was a crime scene over here, but as he was pulling out his phone, he heard a door open, a stirring in the outer office...movement...as though a small wind were disturbing quiet anonymity. Devlin.

He stood for a moment in the doorway, projecting his substantial girth into view of the entire office. It was a look that required more than a casual glance: a soft brim hat framed a fat, firm face while his shirt, tie knot loosened and askew, held a coffee stain and his pants, once ironed, now crumpled. He looked as though he had wandered in from sorting a garbage bin. But while the secretaries and workers were looking at him...and judging...he was taking in their world... the space, the tone, the mixed scents at cross currents in the doorway, the varying looks of horror and the equanimity of some who simply accepted that the Dean was dead. What was the prevalent tone, he asked himself and he answered, "shock". Didn't see much heartbreak, no sign of emotional shattering, not a glimpse of satisfaction (that was important). Just shock.

Well, o.k., he thought. Everyone here seems pretty distraught they lost their boss, not that they lost the person who was their boss. He stepped forward.

"So, who is thinking that the Dean's death is a homicide?"

Dottie Zoster spoke up. "I...I just blurted that out when I called 911, officer. Doris agreed with me. The Dean has been so vigorous lately, it just didn't seem possible that she could have just up and died."

"Any reason to think anyone had a motive?"

"Well, no...I mean faculty and deans argue a lot and she has been involved in some intense curriculum changes...but murder...oh, no. No one I could name would want the Dean dead."

"Well," he sighed, "Where is she?"

Dottie turned to the Dean's office and escorted Devlin in.

"This her?"

"Yes," Dottie answered. "Everything's untouched since I found her."

"Dottie," Devlin spoke, "I'm gonna go over and inspect the body. If I have any questions about general conditions and such, I'll ask you to fill me in. Good with that? Please just remain standing in the doorway. You o.k. with that, Bill?" White nodded.

Don't touch anything, Dottie. Just let me look and answer my questions to the best of your knowledge."

"Of course."

Devlin approached the desk, trying to sample nuance, allowing his nose to test air as he moved closer to the Dean's body...nothing of decay yet...but he found the slightest hint of perfume, something flowery, he thought, just floating in the still air. He noted the cup of coffee resting on her desk, full, now cooled, no lipstick on the rim.

Saw a hearing aid insert on the desk, along with a small white ring flower…no pin on it…maybe a creative gift from someone. Saw her closely cropped hair, sturdy and mixed grey. Looked at her lips. Didn't wear any color. Her head tilted forward revealing a small spot of something at the nap of her neck. No bruising. Walked slowly around the desk and took a good look at Sallie Drake as she had arranged herself in her last moments of life. Natural posture, hands folded with one over the other, the latter wearing some kind of brace. Previous injury he guessed.

He turned to Dottie, "She carry around some kind of handicap?"

"Oh, yes. She had a bad bicycle accident a year ago or so. Has a damaged knee, a crippled right hand, hearing loss in her right ear and she lost an eye. They bothered her…sometimes a lot…but she tried to minimize them as much as possible. Marvelous strength of character."

"How about her relationships with the staff…and faculty?"

"Our staff adores her…well, adored her. Faculty in general were still assessing her policies, and some of them were generating a bit of heat. But you know how that is…new leadership…new ideas… change. People don't like it."

"Well, I'm not sure that I do know about all of that here in a university. Hard to believe anything could get people really upset, maybe just passing irritations with ebb and flows of teaching, eh?"

"Well," Dottie paused, "I guess I could say that the Dean had some curriculum changes in mind. There were some chairs who were very…and I mean VERY…upset about those. Lot of shouting in here yesterday, and lots of comings and going from different department chairs."

"Oh," Devlin paused. "Any security cameras in the office area, hallway?"

"Hmmmmm." Dottie paused, "Well, the office asked for one

several months ago, but tech support hasn't gotten around to installing one. So, no."

Devlin continued to survey the space around the far reaches of the room, slowly turning his body in a slow arc, leaving Sallie Drake undisturbed in the swivel chair where she sat, settling a little more as time passed. He noted that her right leg seemed a little askew... the injury? He squatted down and looked up into her face. White, unmarked, no bruising, one eye, her right, the bad one he guessed, slightly open. He asked Dottie to invite Coroner White to come in.

"Whose doing the autopsy, Bill?"

"Derek Jackson."

"Know him well?"

"Very."

"Is he gonna tell us what happened or what he guessed happened?"

"He will tell us what he knows."

"Good. You know, Bill, the only thing I can see here is that she was sitting in her chair, probably looking out at the view and seized up. The scene is undisturbed, but Dottie tells me she saw a few people throughout the morning. I'm gonna talk to them all, but if it's a benign autopsy, and they don't have anything to speculate about, then I can't see any immediate problem here. Go ahead and cart her away. Tell Jackson to get at her as soon as he can. Case like this, everyone wants to be reassured as soon as possible. No one wants to think this is anything but a sad, untimely death."

"We'll get her under refrigeration right away. What's your next thought?"

"I'm gonna spend a little more time with Dottie and learn what I can about the comings and goings of faculty yesterday, a time when, she says, there was a lot of shouting and swearing in here."

"Doesn't sound very academic," White smiled.

"Not at all," Devlin grinned. "What could possibly matter that much? Still, might be something there."

"Well, there's just one thing I want to know for sure," White said, as he moved to leave.

"What's that?" Devlin asked.

"Is this homicide?"

Devlin grinned, "Well, if its not, I get to go home early tomorrow."

White smiled, "I know. I know."

He ambled out of the office. Devlin turned toward Dottie Zoster and gave her some instructions.

"Please have everyone who saw the Dean yesterday morning, prior to your finding her dead, come in tomorrow. I'll interview them from the Dean's desk. I'll need someone to take notes. You available or should I drag someone in from headquarters."

"Oh, I'd love to help, Detective."

"Done."

Devlin got up, looked around again, lingering on Dottie and her face. Any reaction there...any distress beyond the usual? Nothing. Well, she'd be useful and he'd record everything anyway. Maybe her being there would make the interviews go more smoothly or maybe it would provoke an unrehearsed reaction, maybe from her. Maybe.

He turned and walked out of the office, mumbling, talking to himself.

CONFESSION

Devlin moaned, rolled to his left, dragging a blanket around him, reset his head on the pillow and searched for a new sleep cycle. He didn't find it. Rather, he heard Geraldine's voice softly probing his thoughts.

"Chester, hey there. This is your big, big day, hon. Gonna solve a question...murder or natural death. Right? And now, it's time for you to get your adorable, fat ass out of bed and head for the shower. I've got breakfast ready to hit the grill as soon as you are dressed. Time to take a second cup of coffee. But...you gotta get moving now, sweet darlin'."

He heard her. Grimaced into his pillow, moaned and gave her what she wanted. "Got it, Maizie. Got it. I'm on my way."

Satisfied, Geraldine headed back to the kitchen, waited to hear the shower running and started mixing up pancake batter. Thirty minutes later, shaved, scented, dressed and smiling, Devlin walked into the kitchen.

"What!" He smiled. "Aren't those cakes on the griddle yet?"

"They're gonna be ready before you hoist yourself into your chair...table's all set."

Devlin grunted approval, sat down, began draining the coffee she set before him. Let his mind wander through what he hoped would be a tidy, though dramatic conclusion to a homicide. Four faces laid eyes on Dean Sallie Drake during the morning that she died. Four persons, each of whom might testify as to when she was last alive. One might be guilty. Three others might be able to identify a killer.

"Hmmm. Coffee's great, Maizie. Gotta say this is gonna be a big morning. Can't believe I'll get any dramatic confession, but I should be able to confirm that she died a natural death."

"Can't take that to the D.A., Chester. He's gonna want more than your judgment."

"Oh, sure, I think Derek Jackson, will give us the final answers, but I may be able to guide him a little if I have good conversations with these people."

"How many?

"Four."

"They know her well?"

"Without doubt...department chairs and her secretary. When I know what they know, I'll know it all."

Devlin took the last of his coffee, rose and turned toward the door, patting Geraldine on her bottom as he passed.

"Careful there, tough guy."

"Aren't I always, eh?"

She smiled the look that always warmed his view of the world. He gave her a wave, slipped out the door and headed to the college. He'd settle in to the Dean's office and wait for the autopsy report. The next step would depend on what it told him.

He drove over to campus, parked in the Dean's spot with his police decal plastered in the window. Walked up to the college office, marveling a bit how Sallie Drake must have struggled to get up those stairs every morning. Tough cookie. Continued down Main Hall and softly entered the AL&S suite of offices. Dottie welcomed him with a smile, rose and brought him the list he had requested, "These were the Dean's visitors yesterday morning," she stated.

Devlin took a look, without comment, went into Drake's office.

Sat in a chair replacing the stained one she had recently occupied. He took in the atmosphere, vaguely uncomfortable, feeling Drake was still sitting there, looking over his shoulder.

He looked up, paused. "Dottie...that what they call you, eh?"

"Yes, I answer to that anywhere on campus."

"So, on this list you gave me, the three names that saw Dean Drake yesterday morning...are they regular visitors or do some of them just show up at different times?"

"Well, I would say we have seen the three of them a lot recently because of the curriculum changes Dean Drake was proposing. Each of them wanted to see her yesterday, though I'm not sure what they had in mind...can't believe it was murder, and she seemed to be napping most of the morning. They left without actually speaking to her, I think. I asked them all to come today to the conference room about 9:00 a.m. and wait to be called, Detective. So no rush."

"Fine, Dottie. One thing. Please just call me Devlin...saves a lot of words and formality is not my style. O.K.?"

"Well, certainly, Detective...ahh...Devlin. My goodness. That seems so awkward to say."

"I'm fine with it, Dottie. You'll adjust.

"I'll try hard, Mr. Devlin."

"O.K., then. Let's sort through these visitors. Three of them, eh?

"Yes, Mr. Detective."

He smiled. "You sit in the far corner, Dottie, and take your notes. I'll run a tape recorder from the desk here."

"Pleased to help, Mr. Detective Devlin. Ahh...I guess I'll just ask and see if Suzanna is there. We could start with her?"

"Good."

Ludlow walked in quietly, featuring that soft sway that seem to accompany her every stride. She look about, saw the chair in front of

Devlin's desk and sat down. "How can I help you Detective...Devlin is it?"

Devlin began a soft narrative, recalling what he knew of yesterday's events, indicating that Suzanna was sitting there because she was one of only four people who saw the Dean the morning she died. He trimmed his soft narrative with occasional piercing looks at his "witness", letting her soft tones lull him a little. Suzanna held back nothing about her relationship with Sallie. "It was an intimate relationship," she stated, "and it started early. We kept it both secret and intense. I loved her and I loved every minute of my time with her."

But the longer she talked, the more the small warning bell in Devlin's head began to jangle a little louder. She told an excellent story...yet she seemed inordinately nervous. An artist, he reminded himself...and one not used to harsh pressured conversations...loud, obscene ones maybe, but not quiet pressure.

He pushed back against her narrative. Reminded her that she was the last person to see Drake before Dottie discovered the body. Asked her to repeat her account, asked about the Camellia, a small ceramic ring which Suzanna identified as hers. Devlin asked about locations where they had spent time together the past few months, finally shared information he knew would unnerve any amateur.

"So, Suzanna, your visit was brief, non-disturbing and after a quick inspection you were convinced that Dean Drake was napping and you just walked out with a plan to visit her the next day, right?"

"Yes."

"What if I were to tell you that at the Chancellor's request, Digital Technology recently installed a hidden, micro-security camera here in Dean Drake's office. He had some worries about reactions to the policies she planned to implement throughout the college."

Dottie gave a start, glanced at Devlin, but said nothing.

Suzanna gasped softly, looked away as a crimson flush rushed to her cheeks. There was a silence...10 seconds...another 10...then she hung her head, slowly began to speak again.

"I'm so sorry."

"Oh?", Devlin said softly. "About what? Something more you would like to add?"

She took a breath, held it. Exhaled slowly then began.

"When I went in, Sallie was sitting in her chair, with her back to me. I wanted to confront her about her commitment to me. As I have said, we've been lovers since the first week she became the Dean, and we had pledged to be exclusive partners. When I learned that was not true, I just wasn't going to accept it...really, after all I had given, all I had invested...I just wasn't going to have it."

"So what will we see happening on our video, Suzanna?"

"I walked up to her...you'll see that... to talk to her softly. Didn't think she would be napping, but I was prepared. I take medicine to help control my irritable bowel, and I knew from warnings, and from Shakespeare that it could be easily concentrated into a liquid poison... what the Bard called 'hebanon'."

"She was in a deep sleep, her head slumped a little to the left. The more I looked at her, the more I thought about her betrayal, and I just would not live with that. Shakespeare murdered King Hamlet with ear poison, and it pleased me to think about getting rid of her with a theatrical device. I poured the vial into her ear, quietly, gently. I figured it would penetrate and make her deathly ill, maybe kill her immediately. I didn't care which. She didn't move, so I knew she was in deep sleep, something I was used to seeing after we spent time together. But she wasn't in my bed now, was she?"

She paused, looked away from Devlin, drew a deep breath and exhaled with the comment, "She surely got what she deserved. Can't say I regret doing it. Maybe I'll think differently in a month or two."

"Gotcha' on first strike...yeah, you'll think differently...after ten years in prison," Devlin thought.

He took a deep breath, turned and asked Dottie to go out into the corridor and instruct the on-site patrolman to come in and escort Suzanna Ludlow to jail. He'd have a lot more to learn from her...but later. Looked around again...empty space...but two more suspects to visit. Maybe there was more to the Dean's death they could help him understand.

Dottie escorted David Corrigan into the office. The conversation went quickly, as Devlin began by simply motioning to the corner of the room with his head. "Concealed camera, Corrigan. We're pretty sure we know what happened yesterday. What's your view of it all?

Stunned, Corrigan asked, "What the hell did Suzanna say?"

"She said it all," Devlin replied. "Care to tell me what we're going to find on the video."

"What is it that you think you know, Detective?"

Devlin paused. *"He's defensive...something to hide? Let's find out."*

"We know what you did."

Silence...and it grew to nearly a half minute. Corrigan finally took a deep breath and began.

"Detective, I'm gonna tell you a story."

"I'm pleased," Devlin smiled.

"Yesterday, when I came into to see Sallie...Dean Drake...I did so with plans to kill her...both for the curriculum changes she was going to impose on my department...and for her sexual abuse...of me."

Devlin raised an eyebrow. *What is there about faculty and sexual abuse? Shake hands and they look askance. Look at their bodies and they holler "invasion". Touch a shoulder and they are charging assault. Oh, to see them in a street bar sipping brews and being jovial. Hard to imagine. They're so sensitive. But he never heard a guy holler out about it...never charged a woman for manhandling her companion.*

"Want to elaborate on that, Corrigan?"

"Which part?"

"Sexual abuse."

"Well, sure. I recently learned that she was a transgender freak. That, I never knew…would not have touched her if I knew… disgusting to think of screwing a sliced and diced set of sexual organs. Horrific! She deserved a killing for that if for no other reason. But the curriculum issues gave the idea an exclamation point. Call it an academic death, if that suits you."

"So, you killed her?"

"I believe I did."

"How?"

"You'll see it on the video. I walked around the desk when she seemed to be napping. She was very still, and I used a ultra-thin needle and small syringe to inject her between the ring and pinky fingers on the twisted hand. I believe her injury made that part of her body almost numb. I just needed to put an end to her ugliness."

"What did you inject?"

"Pyraclostrobine."

"Pyra…what?"

"It's a poison. Kills frogs…and quickly. I figured it would work."

"And when you left?"

"Oh, she was alive…but she wouldn't be for too long…doesn't take long for it to find its way into the bloodstream."

Devlin paused, let the silence grow, sorted through his thoughts. *Two killers! We're they collaborating. We're they part of a trio? Was Sallie Drake the honey for a stream of ants?* He read Corrigan his rights and sent him off to jail. Wonder what the next one will say.

"Bring in this Emma Watson, please, Dottie."

Emma walked in, edgy, guilty, conflicted.

She looked at Devlin. He seemed calm…as though he knew

something she didn't. She sat politely, heard him speak to information he had and told her of the camera set up in the corner of the room. She glanced around, didn't see anything.

"It's concealed," he reassured her, "But tell me what happened when you came into the room, Emma?"

Her mind began to spin. He would soon know. Might as well make it as benign as possible.

She paused, that began haltingly, "I popped in and...brought her some coffee. I took a couple of sips, lowered the level...then filled it again... with anti-freeze. Sat it on the desk. As I hoped, it looked filled to a natural level.

Turning, she commented, 'You make a great coffee, Dottie'."

Dottie nodded appreciatively. Devlin wanted no more of that, and cautioned Dottie with his eyes and a slow shake of his head.

"Why would you do this, Emma?"

"She was going to destroy my department and my life's work in the name of pursing her own career, and I wasn't going to let her do that. Just wasn't. The anti-freeze might kill her or at least make her so sick she would have to take a leave. I knew she couldn't taste it...it's so sweet it would fit right in with the flavoring. Anyway, that's what I did. But when I left, she was still dozing. I doubt she ever heard me come in or leave. But that coffee...it would kill her."

"Sad, very sad, Emma, that you've destroyed your career and likely lost your freedom, eh? Going to send you off to jail. Give your lawyer a call right away. They may suddenly be in short supply."

Once Emma was escorted from the Dean's office, Devlin just continued to sit in his chair, looking about the room wondering a bit whether faculty were perhaps a little too sensitive about status, about love, about teaching, about everything. Not one of these killers was going to lose their jobs from anything that Dean Sallie Drake did. She could not hire and fire at will, and they would all be safe in their work and in their lives. Yet they all three attempted homicide...don't know yet which one killed her, maybe all three poisons did it together...eh?

Lost in thought, he continued to ponder the different but lethal actions that killed Drake, and caught himself. There was still one more suspect. He turned to Dottie, and asked her.

"So, Dottie, what were you doing in there?"

"I just went in to check on the dean...*she paused, thought about the camera that had recorded everything...but nothing there would shame her or make her uncomfortable.* I didn't see anything unusual. As the others have reported, her full coffee cup was in place on the desk, *ClearBo* solution there, hearing aid next to it, two folders on the big committee meeting coming up, no sign of any unusual posture in the dean...but she had been napping for quite a while. And yes, there was a small white, ceramic ring on her desk...looked like a Camellia with little flares supporting it...never saw that before. Anyway, I went around the desk and gently touched her shoulder...she was like a sack of sand...just plopped there and then I took a look at her face, tried to time her respiration and realized I couldn't. She wasn't breathing. That's when I called 9-1-1."

"What is this *ClearBo* you mention?"

"Oh, it's a new, special lotion that the dean used to clean her acrylic eye and lubricate the orb tissues holding it in place. That empty socket got dry sometimes and was really irritating. I kept looking for liquid relief and that seem to work best, *ClearBo*."

Devlin eased himself into the chair a little deeper. Dottie's story hadn't changed. She seemed calm, unworried, simply disturbed by the loss of her boss, as she should be. He looked at her, looked around the room, looked over the desk. Everything in sight was the way the four suspects had described the scene. But of the three attempts to kill the Dean, which one of them had administered the fatal poison: anti-freeze (Emma); frog-killer poison (Corrigan); henbane (Suzanna).

Anything at all from Dottie? She seemed completely comfortable and open about her actions. What would autopsy find? Picked up his phone and dialed the Coroner's office, asked for Derek Jackson and began speaking as soon as he answered.

Dottie Zoster listened.

"Devlin here. White says you're doing the autopsy...right?"

"Well, yes. I'll be starting in about 15 minutes."

"I've learned some things in my interviews which might help... take some notes?"

"Right away, Detective...just a moment...ready...fire away."

"Well, we have ourselves just a bit of a mystery, doc. I started things off by telling each of the suspect I had access to a hidden camera in the room. Three of them have confessed to killing the dean: one with henbane; one with an injection of frog killer; one with coffee laced with anti-freeze. None knew any of the others were planning a murder, they say, but your bloodwork may tell us if we have one killer or three. If one, I need to know which one did it, cause I don't want to charge them all with murder...their defense lawyers will point to the other two and that'll be the end of a clear answer to who the killer happens to be. Eh? That what you're thinking too?"

"It is indeed, Detective, and you've given me excellent guidance. I'll start out analyzing fluids and then proceed from there. I should have an answer by the end of the day, and you can charge one of them...or perhaps all of them."

"Just one will do," Devlin answered, "But see what the science says. And say, Derek...according to one of my suspects, you may be discovering something you aren't looking for."

"And what would that be?"

"Surprise me."

Jackson smiled. He liked this Devlin guy.

"I'll have some answers at the end of the day, Detective. Will call."

Devlin ended the connection, turned to Dottie, "Did I miss anything there?"

"Oh, I don't think so, Detective. I didn't think Tech had installed the camera, but if its running it will be very valuable...you might have mentioned having the security camera footage available...maybe it would help the M.E.? What do you think?"

"Nah. That camera story was a lie...I thought it would loosen some tongues, and it has. I'll let Dr. Jackson create his own storyline."

Dottie paused, let her thoughts roll on a bit. Devlin wouldn't know with certainty who killed the Dean until an autopsy confirmed stories, or destroyed them. She began to relax. A medical examiner might find out a lot about Dean Sallie Drake, probably shatter Corrigan's wild tale about her being a former man, but nothing was going to point to Dottie herself as a killer. Why should it?

DEAD RECKONING

Derek Jackson, M.D. That's what it said on the front of his door. Inside, seated at his desk, he began to ponder Devlin's comments. How was he, Jackson, going to surprise a homicide detective? On full alert, he called Mike and told him to meet him in the lab. They had work to do.

Gowned, scrubbed, gloved and masked, he asked himself before he made that first inspection of the body, just what was it that Dean Sallie Drake had been up to that would result in her homicide? She worked at a university, for God's sake, not a Wall Street firm, and it was hard for him to imagine how disputes over workplace strategies would lead to death. He remembered a case up at Stanford some years ago when a graduate student in math failed his third try at passing his orals, and calmly went to the bookshelves in the room, brought out a pistol he had stored, "just in case", and shot dead three examining professors. But students had their careers to lose. He wasn't sure even *he* would convict someone whose life profession was destroyed by three, comfortable and possibly arrogant professors who didn't like the answers they heard.

But, he pondered, this wasn't a graduate student lying on his table under a sheet. This was a dean, successful in her work by all accounts, trying to impose some change, offending some, pleasing others, but apparently not satisfying a small triangle of potential killers. "Killers". My God, that was such a harsh word, Jackson thought. And what were they murdering? A woman who was simply trying to inaugurate change. Sensitive people, these faculty.

Enough. He gently removed the sheet over the body of Dean Sallie Drake. He and Mike drew fluid from veins, arteries, bladder, some lymph nodes in the neck and legs. He took some vitreous from the good eye, removed the bad eye and flooded the field gently, collecting the runoff and marking it for separate analysis. He noticed a coating on the inside of the right ear and scraped it for review.

He turned to Drake's skin, mindful that it was the only body organ he could view in its entirely without using a scalpel. He looked over her arms. Smooth, even tone. Apparently she was not outdoors much and he saw no signs of sunburn, lesions or tan lines. He began a closer inspection, beginning at the top of her head, inspecting for indentations, scars, burn marks, or bruises. Stopped at her neck. Some residue there. He scraped it for analysis. Noticed some light scarring on the throat.

Something distinctive in her breasts too, he thought. Looked more closely...scars on her breasts. He touched each piece of flesh separately, and moved them about. Implants...high quality too.

He continued down her abdomen, pressed gently, searching for any pockets of gas or solid matter that might indicate a tumor, continued down to her pubic junction and inspected her reproductive organs for irregularities or infection. He didn't get far. Almost immediately, he saw what now made his cadaver so important to Devlin. This body, born male, had undertaken transgender surgery. What he saw now was erectile tissue from the penis pushed into a pelvic pouch and transformed into a vagina. It was surgically arranged so that part of the head of the penis now became the clitoris. The urethra was clipped and shortened, and the balls sack, empty of testes, were now the major lips of the vagina. He had seen such configurations only twice in the past, but neither had the degree of expertise that he found here.

And this transformation would explain the scarring on the throat, smoothing the Adam's apple. So, Sallie Drake, he thought, you were once a man and now you are not. Wonder if that bothered anyone... lovers, family, associates, friends?

He made his notes, continued on to some of the specific locations that Devlin wanted him to affirm. He ran his hands down each arm inspecting carefully for injection sites and finding none, began to look at the hands. "The right hand, between last two fingers," Devlin had said, was reportedly used as an injection site for what he called "frog-killer".

Jackson took a good, close look with a magnifying glass and found it, as suggested, at the base of the ring and pinky finger. So, someone placed a very thin needle in there, and the Dean, sleeping, might well not have noticed the light prick between the fingers. Given her injury, there was probably a good deal of numbness in the hand anyway. He got a small scalpel and carefully, slowly opened the skin looking for the needle stick, or any pool of poison that might not have been absorbed by the body. He found some.

He went back to the other suspected site, Dean Sallie Drake's right ear. Swabbed it out. Combined with the previous scraping, this was as good a look as he could have without some careful dissecting and he wasn't going to do that. Lab analysis would give him all the answers he needed, but even now, he could confirm two of the suspect's stories.

Now what was the third account? Oh, yeah, she reportedly put anti-freeze in the Dean's coffee, causing death. But, Devlin said, there was no evidence that the Dean drank any of it. He would welcome a finding. Again, Jackson thought, labs would give him answers. He made the Y incision now, lifted the stomach out and sliced it open, looking for signs of severe inflammation from the anti-freeze. Nothing there.

He continued with a look at the Dean's gross anatomy...liver, gall bladder, small intestine...and observed inflammation in all three...puzzling. Nothing Devlin reported being injected into the Dean would account for these flare ups. Jackson opened the lungs and found evidence of widespread, tiny clotting. He sliced into the arteries and veins supplying the heart and found them spattered with red colonies of blood cells. He paused.

This was not a healthy woman.

So, he asked himself...again. What killed her? He spent the rest of the afternoon answering the question, finding one more surprise, and in the late afternoon, he called Devlin.

"So," Devlin's first question came peppering out, "What did you find. Which one of them killed her...or are they all three guilty?"

"I'm thinking of the best way to tell you this, Devlin, so let me go through your shopping list."

"Eh?"

"I'll start with the surprise you promised me. Yes, Sallie Drake was transgender and the surgery that carried her the distance was of very high quality indeed. She must have been very comfortable in her new body, and considering the hormone injections it took to keep her that way, it's no wonder she had such an active sex life...lots of restlessness there I would think."

"Well, she could have fooled me," Devlin commented, "But then again, I wasn't looking too hard. What else did you find?"

"Well, this is the hard part," Jackson said, "We ran lab tests on tissue we gathered from the injection site, from the run off of the irrigation we did from her bad eye, and from her stomach, even analyzed for henbane in the blood tests."

"And...and...and, Christ, Jackson, get to it. What do you know... for sure. No guessing now...for sure."

"Well, for sure, she was dead before any poisons entered her body."

"WHAT!"

IMPRESSIONS

Devlin sat silent, letting the phone rest in his hand, his mind racing through all that he had heard that morning and all that he expected to hear from Mark Jackson. How could it be? Dead Dean...natural causes...but three confessions to homicide. He asked again, "What are you saying, Doc?"

"You heard me," Jackson replied.

"Be careful, here, Doc. What killed her if it were not one of these upset department Chairs?"

"It's actually pretty straightforward, Devlin. She died from a heart attack, and the coagulants were suggestive of what I have seen in reports about blood clots in women taking hormone therapy. Also consistent with a few Covid 19 deaths following vaccinations in older-aged women. I checked medical records and she had been vaccinated a few months ago. None of the ingredients you mentioned to me were found in her blood. We did find some traces of botox in the washings from her bad eye orbit, and that was a bit of a surprise...but again, nothing in her blood. There were surface scrapings of henbane in her ear, but overall, she was clean as a freshly laundered white sheet, and the idea that you have a murderer in custody is gonna fall apart, Devlin. You might charge them all for adulterating a corpse, but that isn't gonna get you any headlines, eh?"

Devlin felt his body begin to shrink. *What in the hell was he going to announce to the public? What was this gonna' mean to the university? A Dean worked herself to death? Unlikely. Christ! And now he had to release his suspects and try to account for arresting all three of them. And how could he do that and still impress the press? Maybe Jackson had given him his way out: hormone therapy and COVID with its long term after effects.*

"You still there, Devlin?"

"I am...and I'm not happy."

"I can understand that...you can have a look at my notes tomorrow and take it from there. From my point of view, I'm done with Dean Drake."

"And so is everyone else," Devlin thought. He thanked Jackson for his work and hung up, his mind racing.

Complicated...but maybe that was a good thing. Explaining the Dean's death would require more than a typed news release. He needed to reach out to the press, meet with reporters personally, bring them into the diagnosis as colleagues and let them write their stories. Their headlines would cover his stilted explanations, maybe shift focus on to the M.E., Derek Jackson. If this worked, everyone would go home with what they wanted: a closed case; a medical surprise; sex scandal of sorts; exoneration of faculty; reflective praise for him.

He tried his ideas out on Maizie that evening as she served him supper.

"Chester, I think you're on the right track. The press will go crazy with excitement learning about a transgender dean who is possibly infecting students and faculty with Covid 19."

"Eh, Maizie? How is she infecting them?"

"Her sex life...my God, Chester, she's screwing faculty men, faculty women and my guess is that she was into students too. Heavy breathing meant she was shedding virus loads in all directions, even if she was vaccinated, she could pass the virus to others. Close contact, sex, my God, who knows how many bodies she's been wrapping herself around. Who knows what diseases she was carrying, or how many underage children she was luring into her sex-trap? Anyone try to tap into the social media and see what the chatter is?"

"Social media? Sex-trap? Child abuse?"

"It could be true, Chester."

"Christ, Maizie, I'm not looking for a federal investigation! All I want is proof of her cause of death. Evidence is what I want, Maizie, and that is what I have. She's a tranny; she screwing everything in sight; she's dead from hormone shots and Covid. I just want to make it clear that we were pursuing our due diligence in questioning these faculty people. Guess I could have a sergeant at the station house go through some social media to say we looked for sexual abuse of minors, but I'm not looking much."

"Well, you should...and mention it in your press conference so you'll look like you've covered all your bases. Where you gonna have the meeting anyway?"

"I'm thinking right there in the Dean's office. Let reporters feel like they are "on scene" and give them all the details, top to bottom, so to speak. They'll run with it, and I'll look like I know what I'm talking about eh?"

"That'll work, Chester. Anything else you thinking?"

"Yes. I would like you to gather 3-4 of your women friends and come on down too. More women there, the better. Makes the whole scene a little softer, a little more intimate, maybe help give the press the view that the Dean was a victim of disease, rather than an out-of-control sex maniac."

"Oh, I can do that...love to in fact."

"And Maizie, make them attractive women."

He called Dottie Zoster and asked if he could use the Dean's office as a setting for a press conference, and checked back with Dr. Jackson to see if he and his wife might attend it in a show of scientific consensus to clear all doubt. The more feminine posturing he could arrange, he thought, the more sympathy he might get from the public. *"Well informed detective proves suspects innocent."* That's what he wanted from the press.

Dottie arranged it all. And the next day, before reporters showed up, Devlin had another conversation with her, mentioning the Dean must have been trying botox, the real, pure drug, to improve the presentation of her eye. Dottie reacted with a wide-eyed look of her own, asked Devlin how could they learn anything like that?

"Jackson said the botox he found was not an injected ingredient. Sallie was flooding her eye socket with it and it was in the irrigation run off when they were first inspecting the body. Dangerous stuff," Devlin commented. "It could have travelled into the blood stream and induced a heart attack. Very high concentration. Must have been an adulteration in that *ClearBo* she kept on her desk. You said it came from India, right? Or maybe that's why she bought that brand. Foreign made with natural ingredients. Maybe that appealed to her. Any insight on that, Dottie?"

"Oh, my goodness, Detective, that's a horrible thought. She was quite leery about a product from India to begin with. But she had come to prefer that brand. Must have been adulterated in Mumbai. She said it did a better job of reducing eye socket discomfort...gosh, maybe that was because the botox was part of the ingredients. Gonna have the lab run the bottle through some tests?"

"Yep. I did. The botox is in there...in high concentration...I guess right from the factory. Any other bottles we could sample for contamination?"

"Oh, my, no. That was the last one. I have more on order. But free flooding of botox in her eye? My goodness! Even I know that stuff can spread into the system and kill or paralyze a person."

"Think she might have poured some botox into the bottle to help keep the skin around her false eye a little more wrinkle free?"

142

"Possibly, Detective. Sounds ridiculous if one knows how it works, but sometimes she fixated on what that accident had cost her, and she was no medical expert, that's for sure."

"Well, apparently not. Gotta' say, it's a bitch…to have to medicate all the time just to try to feel normal, and never quite managing it," Devlin commented. "Well, here comes the press and guests. Why don't you circulate around and commiserate with people. I think we can create a professional atmosphere with just quiet talk and a brief statement I'll give to the reporters over there."

He walked to the general center of the crowd, and began making some comments about the weariness of the Dean, "fighting complications from Covid and vaccine side-effects, worn to an edge of collapse." Somewhat uncomfortably, he went on to elaborate Drake's personal challenges in dealing with the injuries from the bike accident. He paused, then with some hesitation and a little embarrassment, he described her "refocused" gender, commented that adjusting to a "new sexual life" and the hormone therapy she had to maintain must have challenged her all the more. Living as a transgender person amidst bitter academic issues could easily have undermined her health, leading to the heart attack.

For most of the gathering, Devlin's report was startling. For others, it was simply informative. Andrea satisfied herself that Derek was comfortable and wandered about the room a bit, picking up an undertone of comments ranging from, "I always thought she was a little different," to the more common question. "Who's going to be the new Dean?" The answer offered most often was simply, "Gotta be the Chair of the English Department…what's her name…Eleanor Rouse. She'll be a surprise change of flavor, for sure, chaos amidst confusion."

Devlin's remarks filtered through the chatter to Dottie's mind like a battering ram. As carefully as she had catered to Dean Drake… reassured her, calmed her, attended to her…she had never imagined her as anything other than the woman she had come to serve. The shouting in her office certainly pointed to a different person than the one she knew, and she had doubted Corrigan's accusation was really true. Now, she knew it was. All of it.

Her boss, her lover, was a freak! And a slut. My God! Their trysts in the auditorium, pearls in her own steady, boring life, were now ruined by infidelity and physical repulse. Dean Sallie Drake had sought her out, seduced her into a deeply committed, sexual relationship and she responded...became intensely bonded to her. She liked being of service, enjoyed being a secretary, especially to a powerful person. Sallie was demanding, insistent, sometimes abusive, but her range of behavior fit nicely into their daily relationship...secretary to superior...and when they were in the auditorium, they were equals. But now, Dottie knew in her heart and in the knot in her belly that she had lost the most intimate partner of her lifetime. She hated Sallie Drake...she was repulsed by Sallie Drake...and she loved Sallie Drake. With waves of sorrow, she missed her. She wanted to sob about Sallie, scream at Sallie, declare her love for Sallie in front of the entire assembly, but all she could utter were little phrased regrets.

Her eyes moistened, even as she commiserated with staff and faculty friends, a tear or two leaking down her face...and as they dampened her cheeks, she noted Andrea Jackson visually sorting through the group with an intensely focused look, coming to linger on her, swiftly looking her up and down. Strange, she thought. She didn't know Andrea Jackson, and to her knowledge neither did any of the rest of the crowd. Dottie grew uneasy and moved into the group of reporters.

Andrea caught Dottie's glances. Some special heat there compared to the body language and sighs coming from the various former suspects Devlin had identified to Derek. Intrigued, she focused on the group more intently, ignoring postures of formal dismay, looking instead for embedded dislike, disgust, even hatred. In her own way, she could unlock the secrets of social judgment and personal regard as well as her husband could assess a bruised liver. This, a social engagement, was her laboratory, and she energized her glances, slicing open the body language of former suspects, catching the false declarations of sorrow, picking up an underlying hostility to Sallie Drake's very existence. She decided attempted murder fit their profiles just fine.

She looked over to Derek, from time to time, smiled, warmed again by his presence in her life. She felt the glow of his attention, almost blushed, but continued to assess the room. And the more she watched, and listened, the more she began to understand some of the tensions surfacing around the life...and the death...of Dean Sallie Drake. When Devlin finished, she gathered her things, waited and walked him to their car.

He seemed deep in thought, finally cleared his throat and broke the silence, "What did you think of that group, hon?"

"I saw a pack of wolves, disappointed the buffalo had died a natural death?"

"Really?"

"Oh, yes...vengeance, anger and a kind of a smug satisfaction... everywhere I looked...well, almost everywhere. I must say this Eleanor Rouse, whom gossip has as the replacement for Dean Drake is a walking swirl of confusion and untidiness. Doubt she will be well regarded by the college. And Dottie Zoster seemed to be having a difficult time. Very much on edge...enough that I could have believed that she was a suspect herself...that would make four."

He paused. Waited for a red light to change, finally commented again.

"You know, Devlin used Dottie as though she were his personal assistant. He must have a lot of trust in her and in what she told him."

"I know, but that may have been a strategy. He sure kept an eye on her as he spoke to different little groups. It's as though she knew a truth that he did not, even though nothing in your autopsy could confirm a murder. Most of the time, she appeared to be fully immersed in the process of remembering Sallie Drake with compassion and some kind of affection, but I'm sure her feelings were far more intense than anything Devlin suspects."

"Didn't you see something like that with the other three?"

"No I didn't, nor from anyone else really."

He thought some about what Andrea was saying, then mentioned one observation he had made that didn't go away.

"You know, hon, if the witnesses are to be believed, two of them were in an intimate relationship with the Dean, and there may have been others, maybe that Burton woman, but no tears there at all. Yet Dottie wasn't in bed with Dean Drake...so far as I know. So why her apparently deep distress. Why was that?"

"*So far as we know* is the operative phrase here, Derek."

"You think she was another lover that Drake was dallying with... that she tried to kill Drake?"

"Well, emotion is a guide to motive, don't you think?"

"Well, maybe...but she was crying."

"Tears from fears or from loss, from release or retribution?"

"Hmmmm, so what do you make of the crying game...was it real or was it show?"

"You want me to assess Dottie's emotional turmoil?"

"Well, sure. Whaddya think?"

"Why she wept?"

"Yeah. Why?"

Andrea paused, reflected as though going through her answer more than once, finally sighed. "She was the only one in that room who loved Dean Sallie Drake."

"Ohhhh? Hmmm. You saying that she and the Dean were lovers? Dottie Zoster was part of the cattle call? Wonder if she knew that?"

"Oh, I don't think she did. Now of course, she does. Had to break her heart in ways that the others, Suzanna and Corrigan, could not feel...or notice, and Emma Burton wasn't shedding a tear, either, not a sniffle. But Dottie was crying about Drake's death because she had lost the love of her life."

"Hmmmpphhh." He remained silent for three more blocks. Finally, he had a response, "Well then, an unlikely suspect, but a suspect nonetheless, I guess."

"She sure is. Jilted lovers have been known to act irrationally, God knows, and deeply regret it."

"Well, could be. Three, maybe four tried, and none succeeded. Wonder what Devlin's thinking about? Dottie?"

Andrea made a small hum, "My thinking is that he has finished the case and would like nothing more than to stay away from the entire university. What about you, sweet man? What are you thinking about Dottie?"

"Well, she's not on my table, so she's not my problem."

"Not today," she laughed, "But she is a lover, no longer innocent, devastated in her loss. Likely she'll recover just fine, and she'll be looking for love...maybe in the wrong places. You might see her under your light sometime."

"Hmmmphhh. Maybe," he smiled, "But I'll slice that apple when I have too."

"Derek! Please," she laughed, "A little respect for our Eve."

He chuckled. Sallie Drake, in the midst of enemies, had escaped them all...natural death."

He drove on, new thoughts skittering, "So, what's for supper?"

"Me."

"I'll have two servings."

Andrea smiled.